CAPTAIN BARBOSA
AND THE PIRATE HAT CHASE

JORGE GONZÁLEZ

Graphic Universe™ • Minneapolis

Story and illustrations by Jorge González

First American edition published in 2019 by Graphic Universe™

Copyright © 2013 by Jorge González and Bang. Ediciones. Published by
arrangement with Garbuix Agency.

Graphic Universe™ is a trademark of Lerner Publishing Group, Inc.

Graphic Universe™
A division of Lerner Publishing Group, Inc.
241 First Avenue North
Minneapolis, MN 55401 USA

For reading levels and more information, look up this title at
www.lernerbooks.com.

Library of Congress Cataloging-in-Publication Data

Names: González, Jorge, 1970– author, illustrator.
Title: Captain Barbosa and the pirate hat chase / Jorge González.
Description: First American edition. | Minneapolis : Graphic Universe, 2019. |
    Summary: Captain Barbosa sails with his trusty shipmates—a mosquito, a
    crocodile, and an elephant—and when a seagull steals his treasured skull hat,
    Barbosa and his crew give chase. —Provided by publisher.
Identifiers: LCCN 2018014449 (print) | LCCN 2018021009 (ebook) |
    ISBN 9781541542709 (eb pdf) | ISBN 9781541541542 (lb : alk. paper) |
    ISBN 9781541545274 (pb : alk. paper)
Subjects: LCSH: Graphic novels. | CYAC: Graphic novels. | Sea stories.
Classification: LCC PZ7.7.G655 (ebook) | LCC PZ7.7.G655 Cap 2019 (print) |
    DDC 741.5/973—dc23

LC record available at https://lccn.loc.gov/2018014449

Manufactured in the United States of America
1-45328-38808-6/5/2018

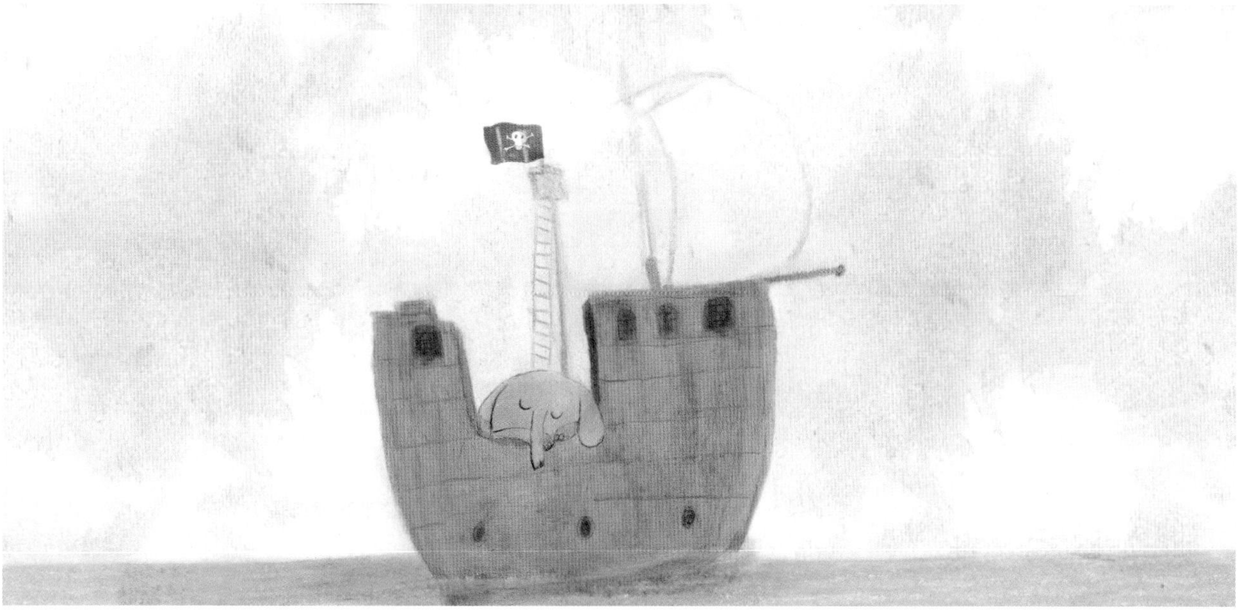

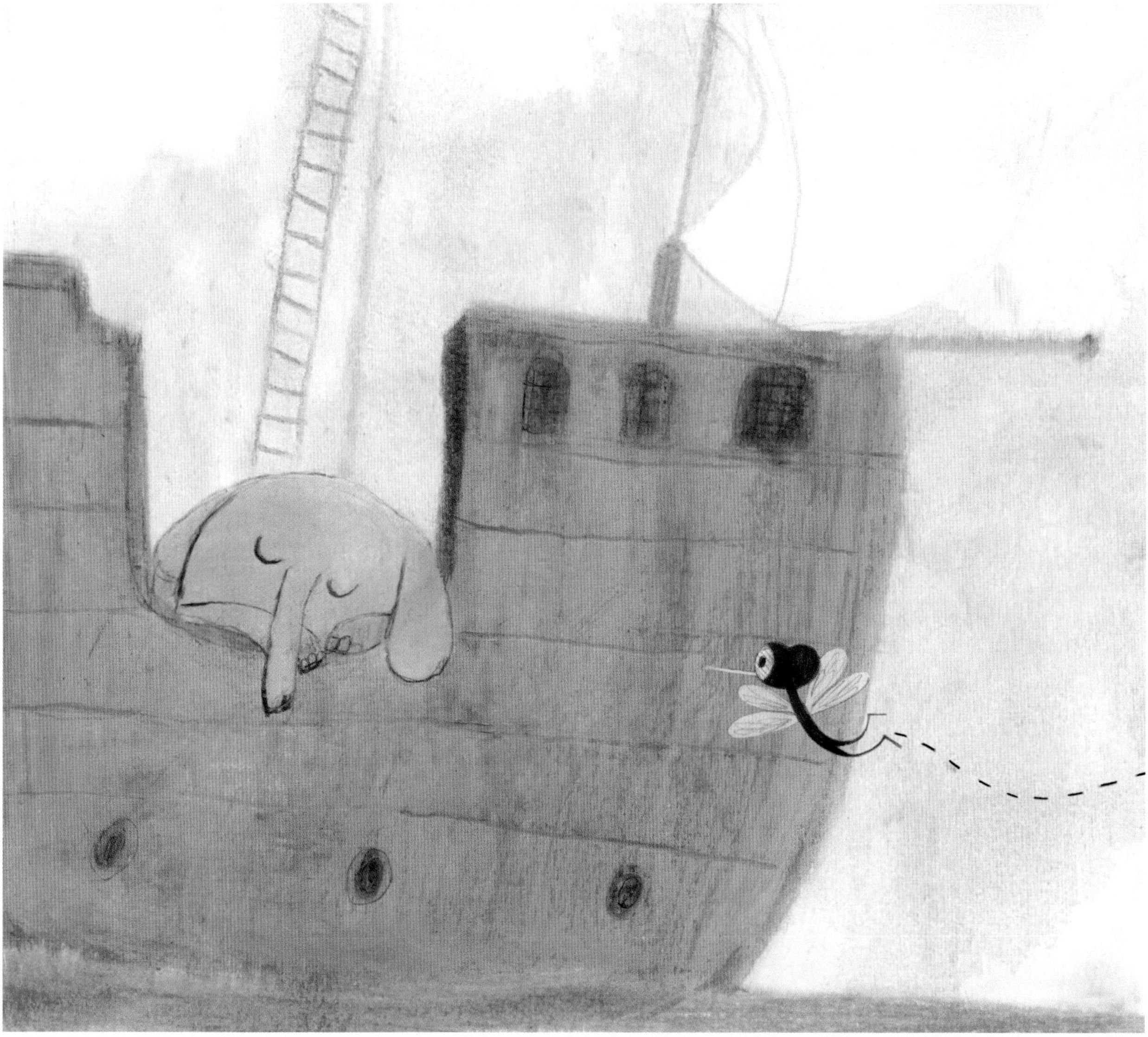

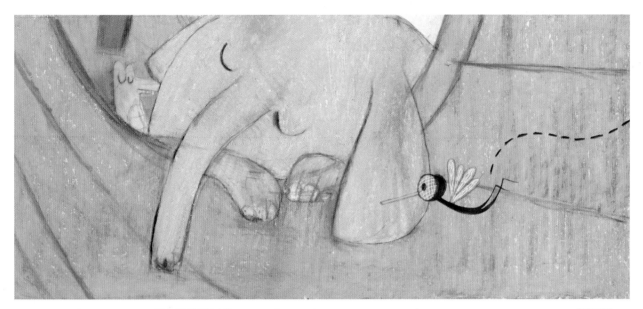

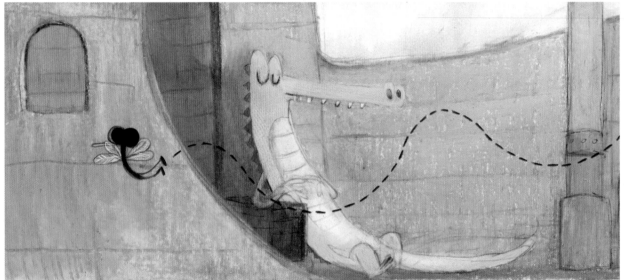

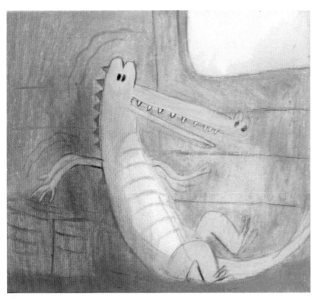

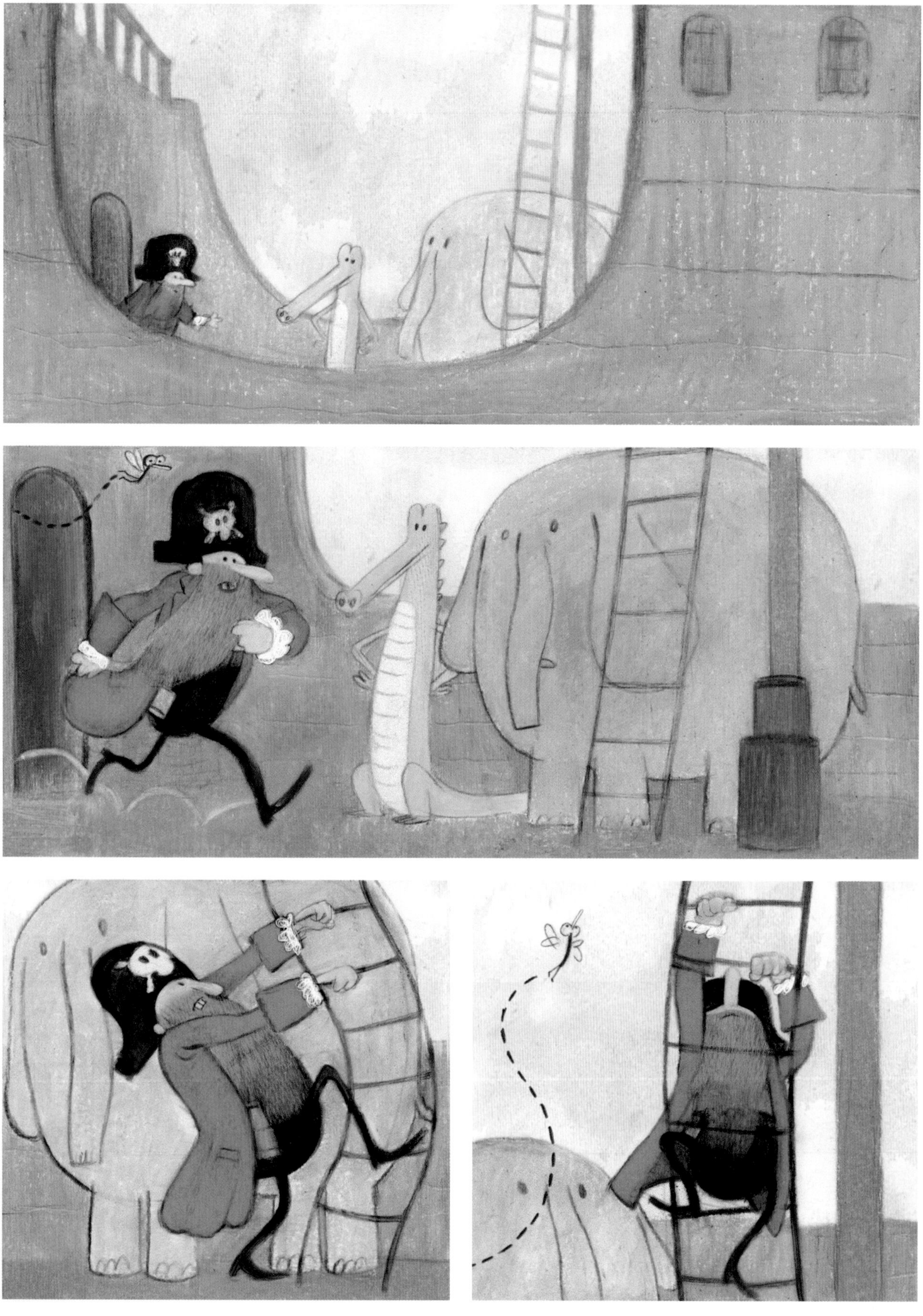

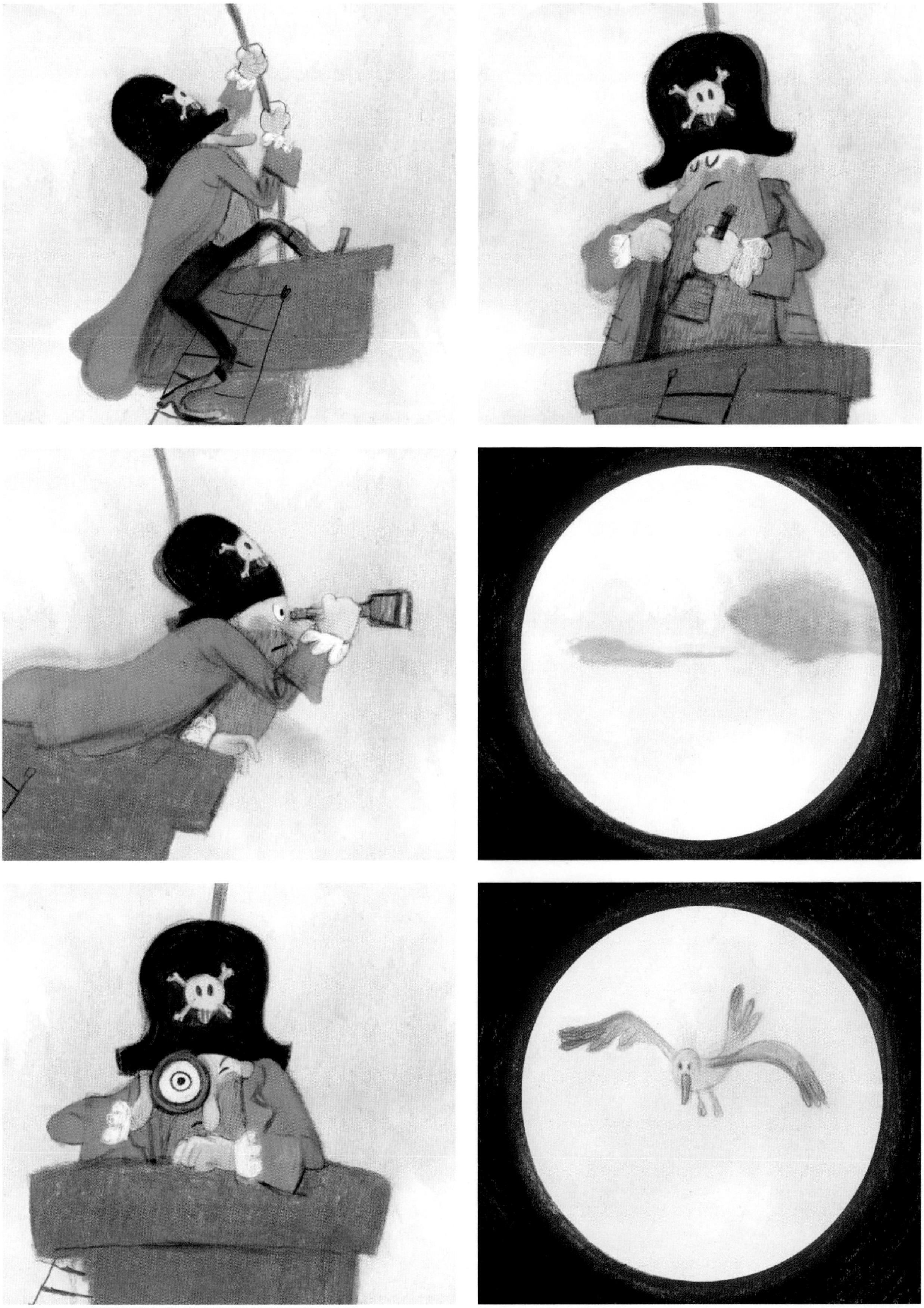

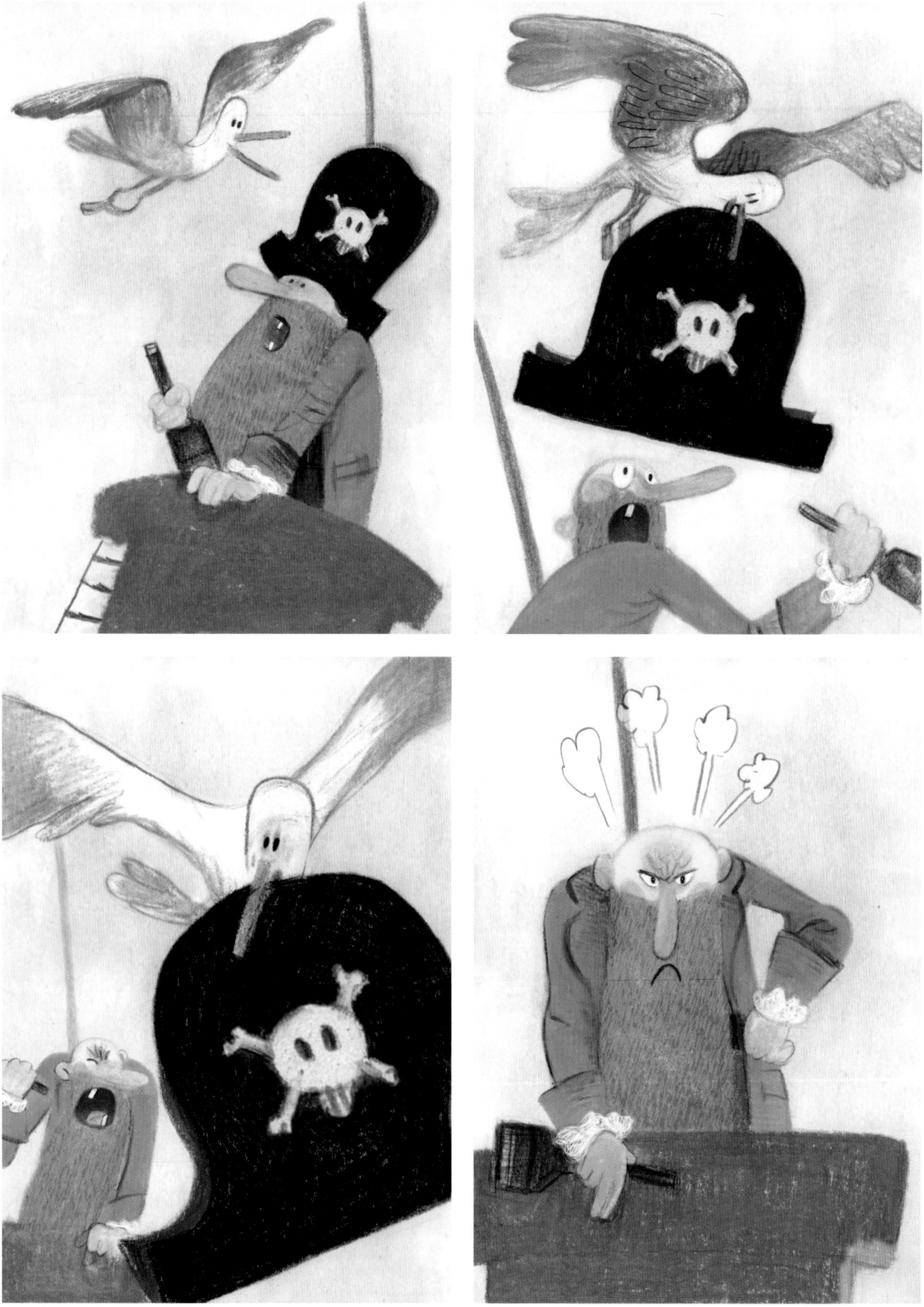

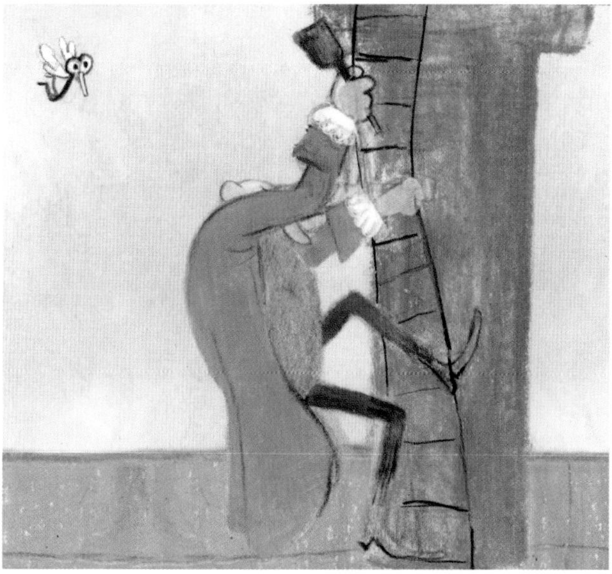

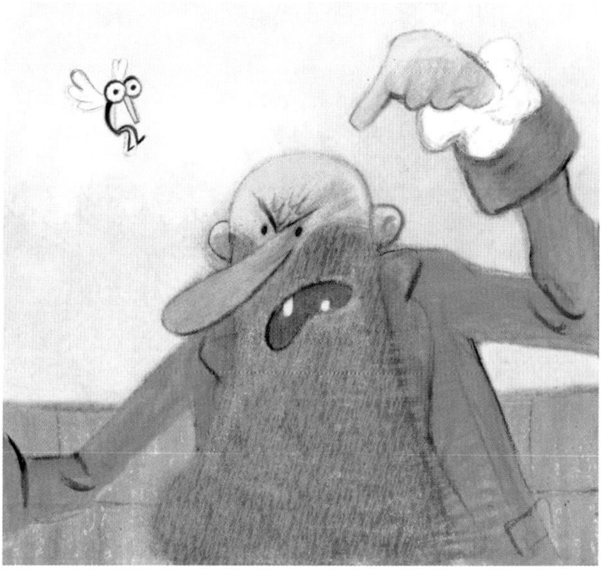

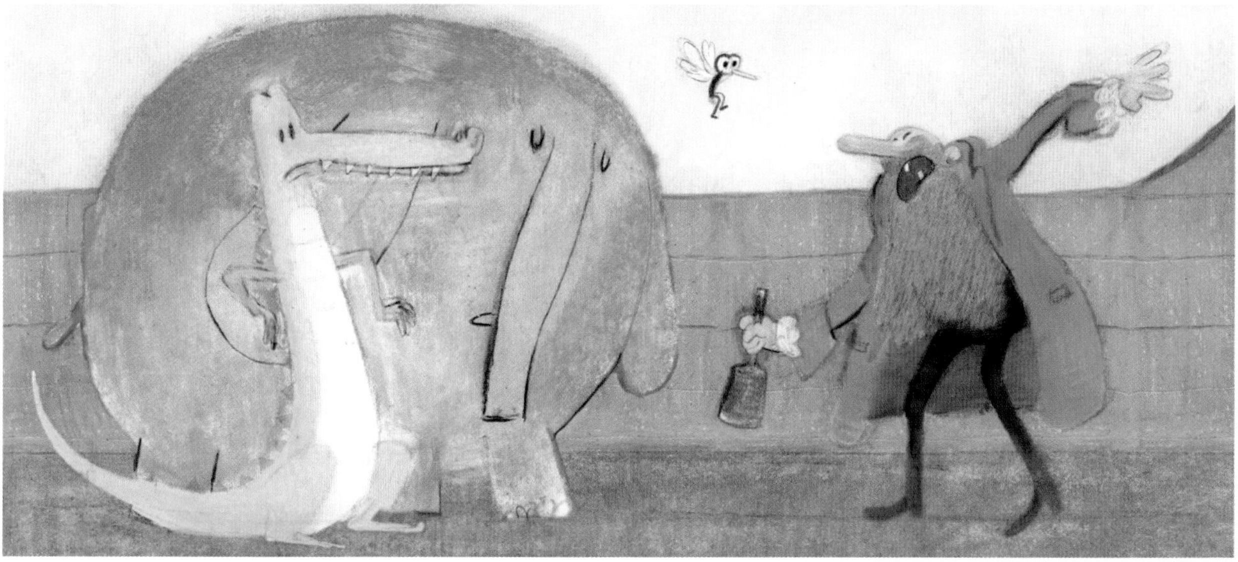

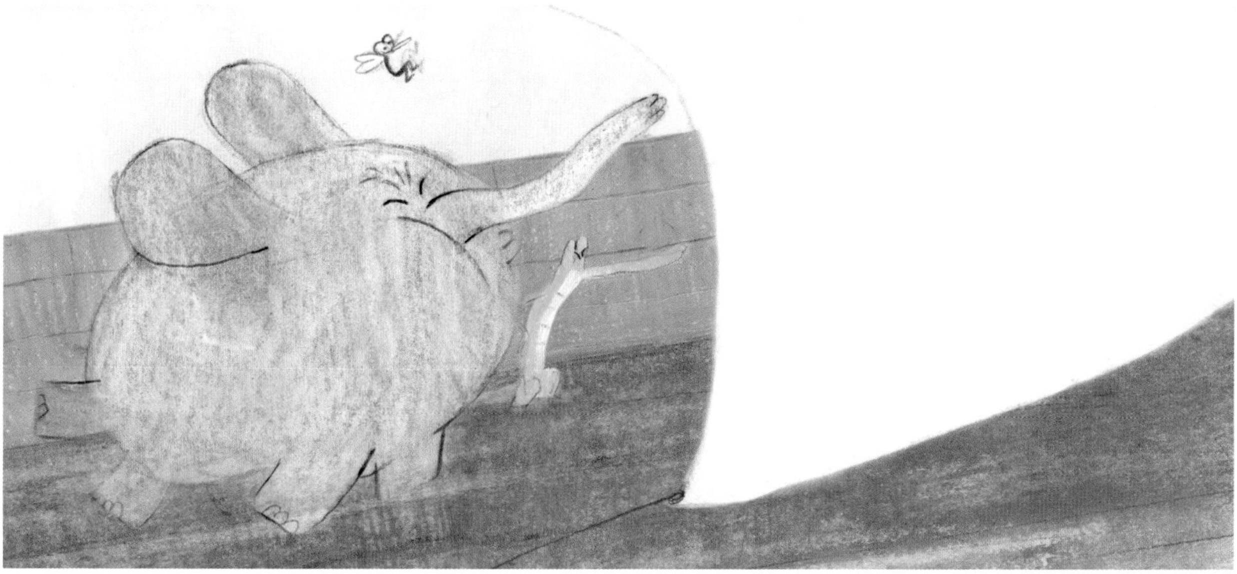

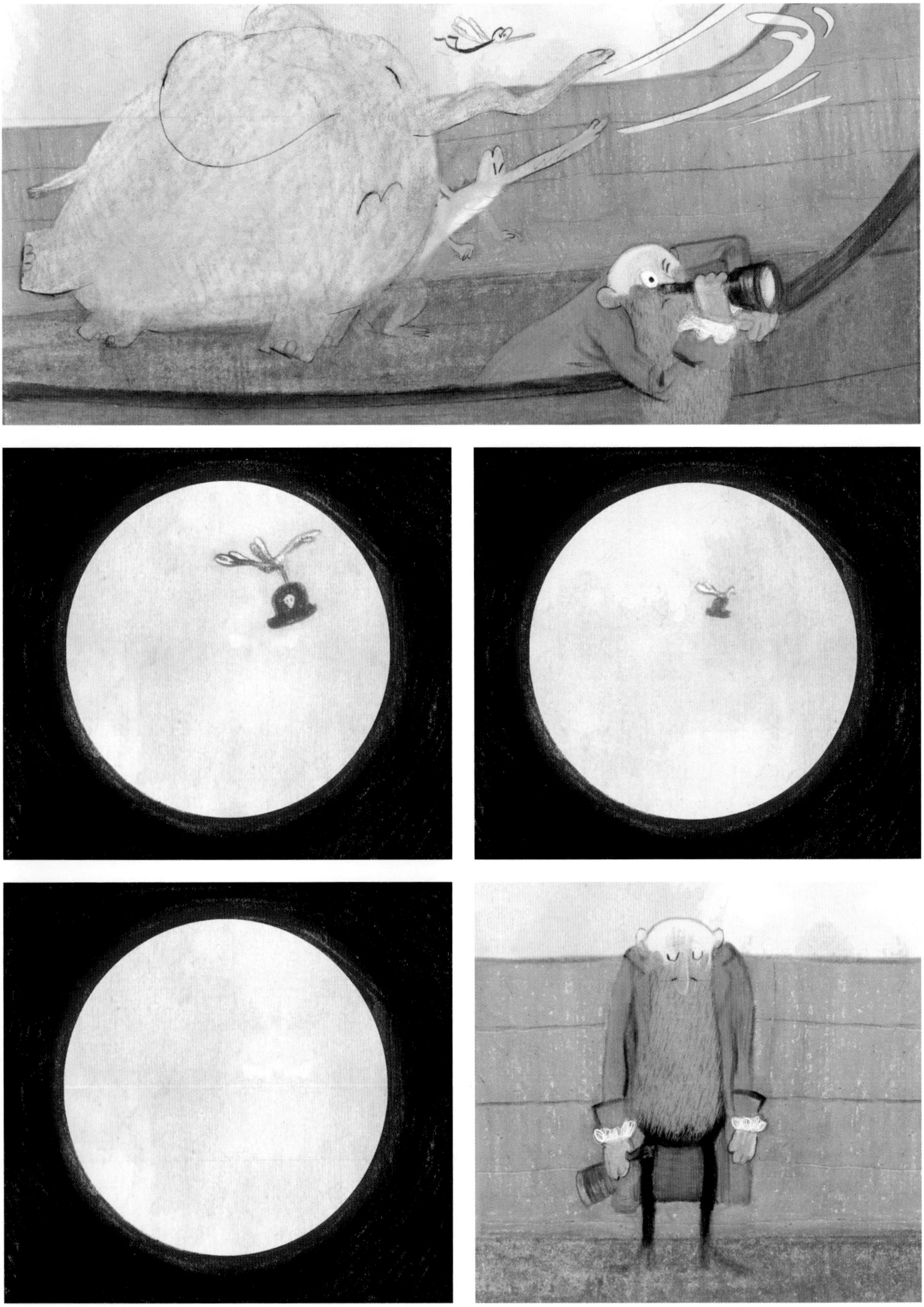

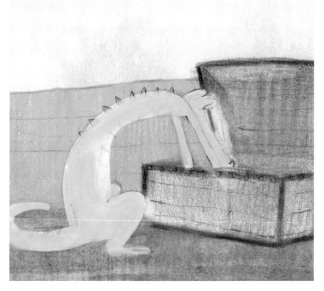

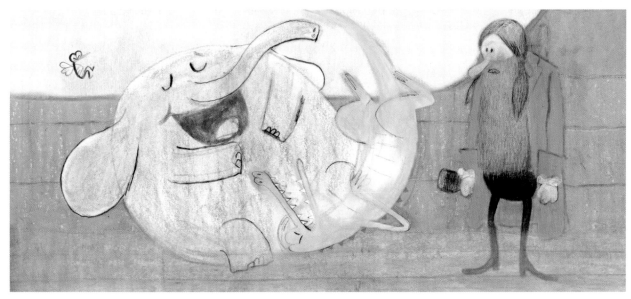

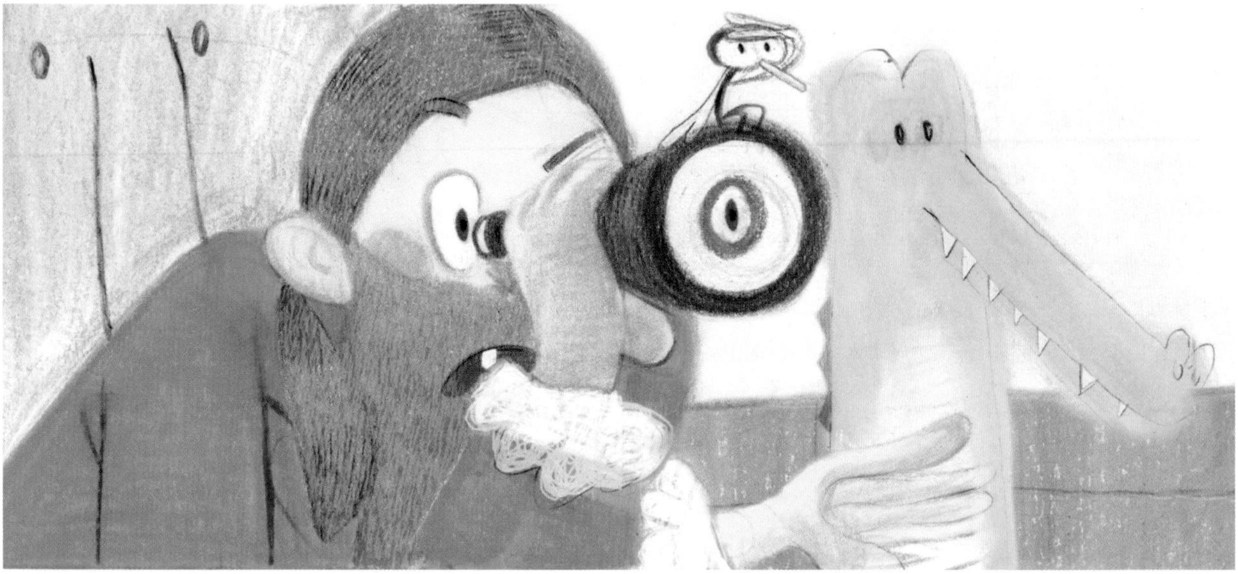

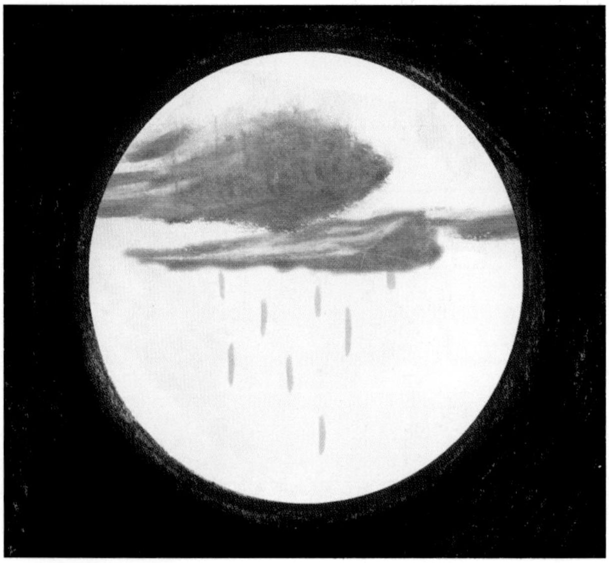

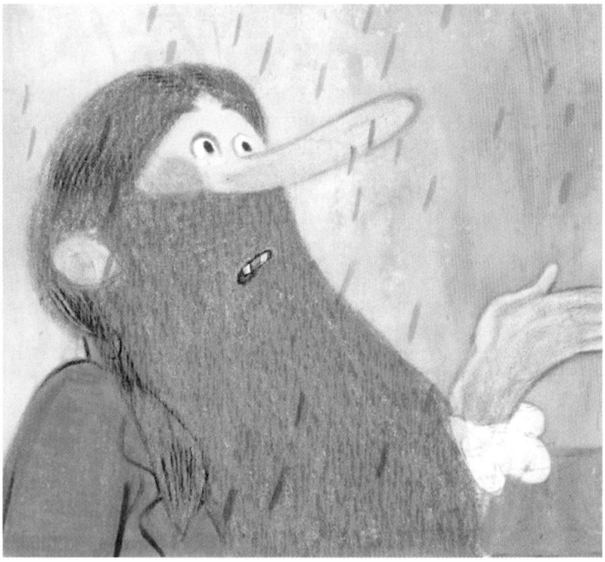

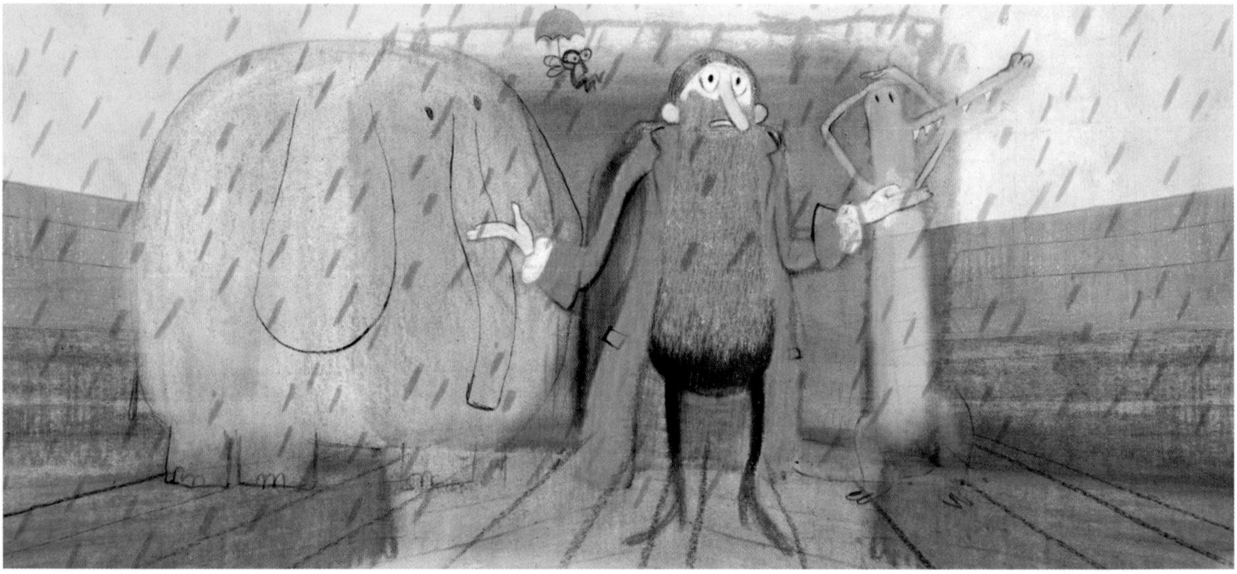

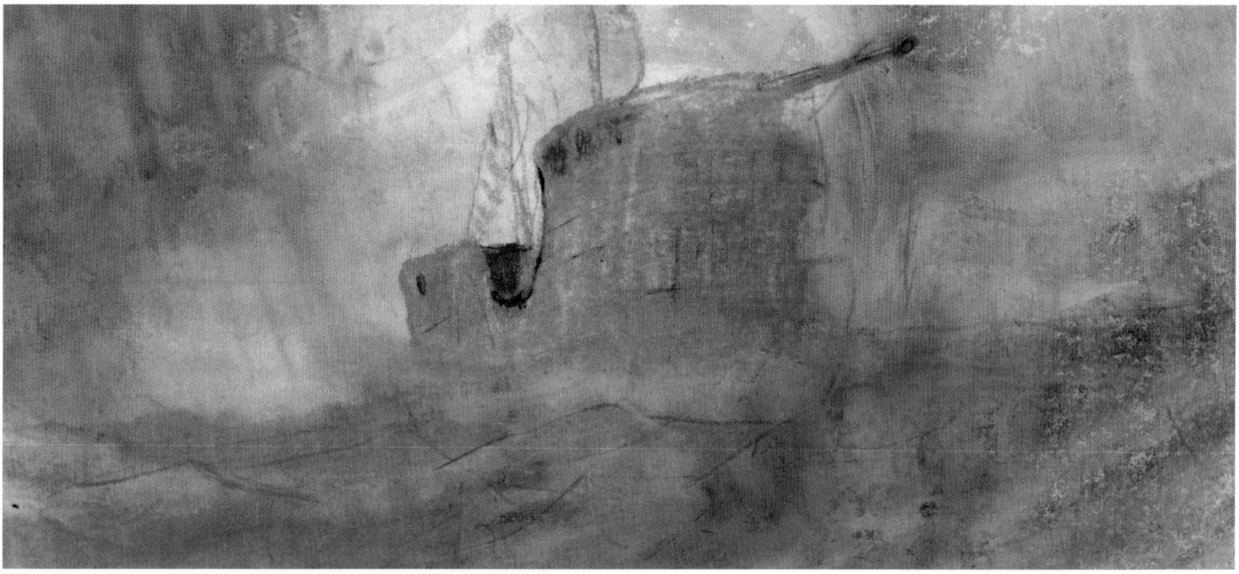

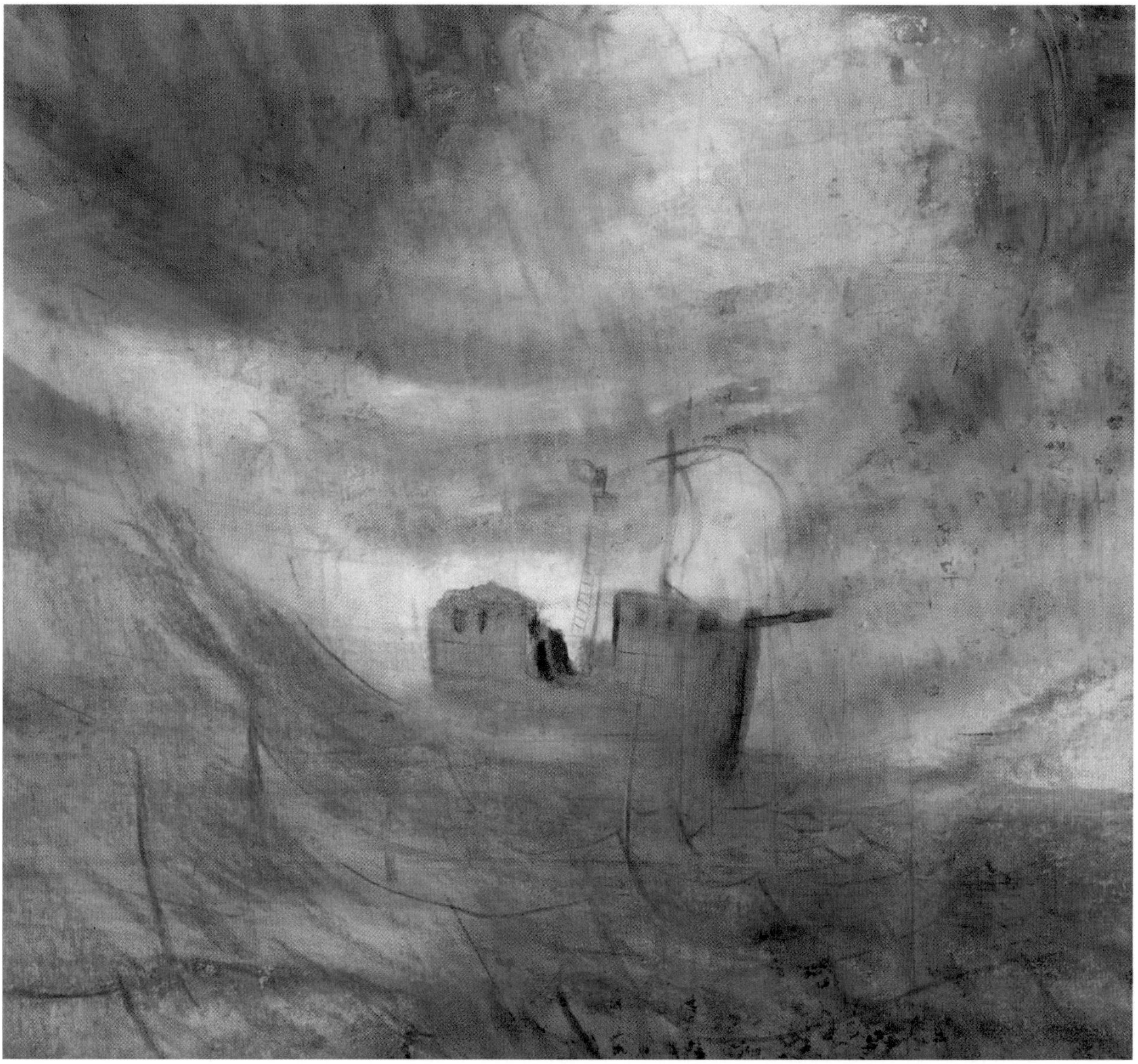

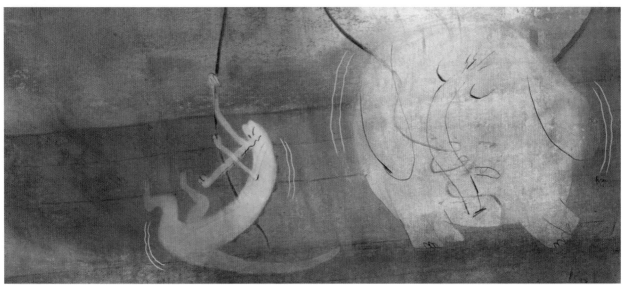
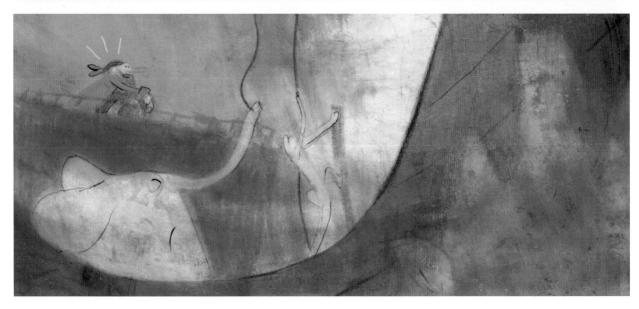

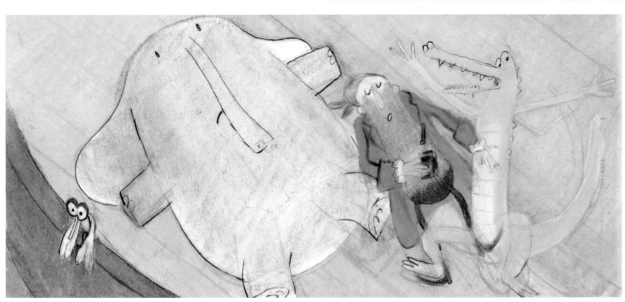

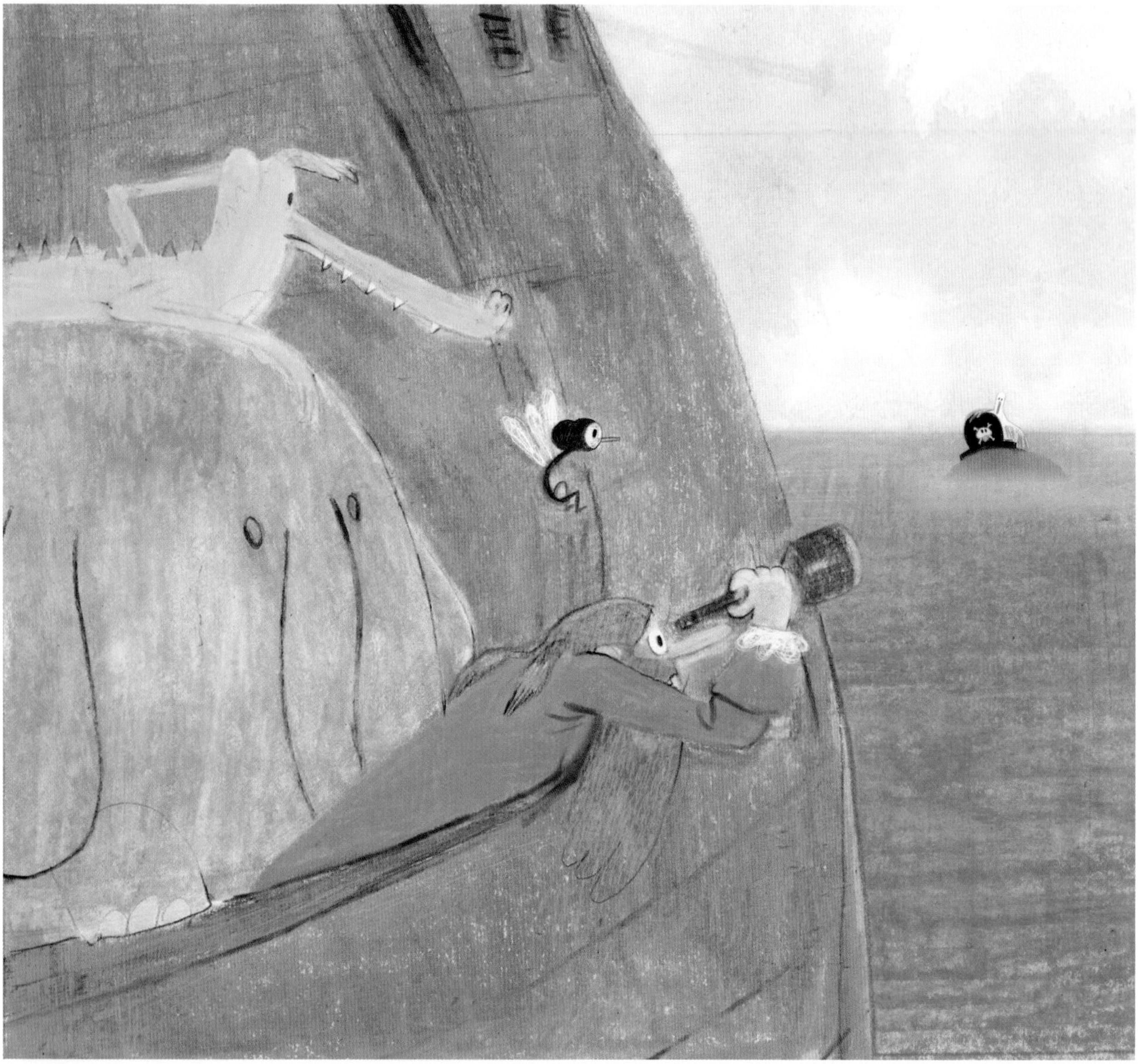

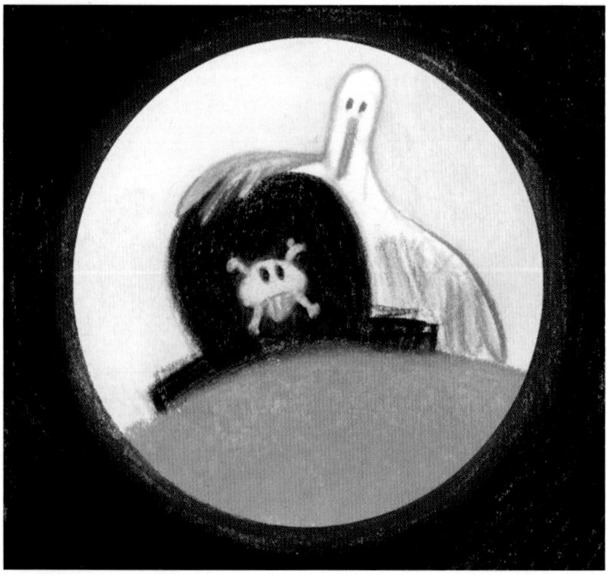

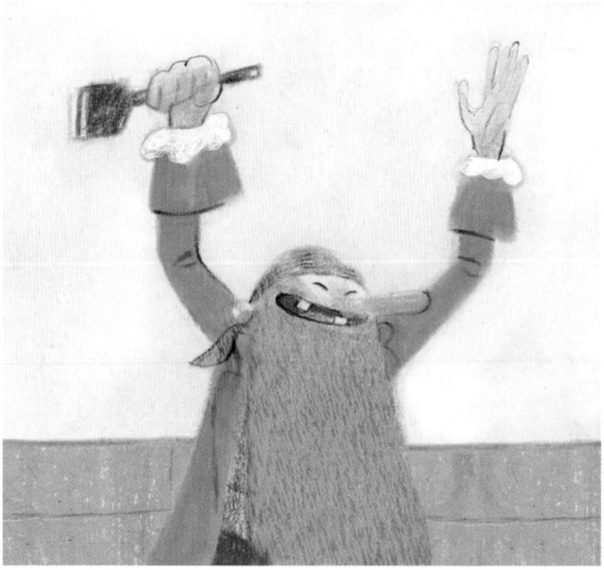

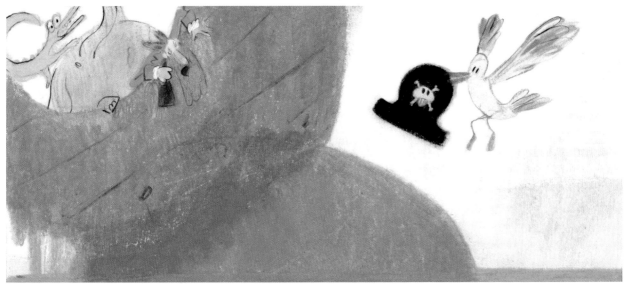

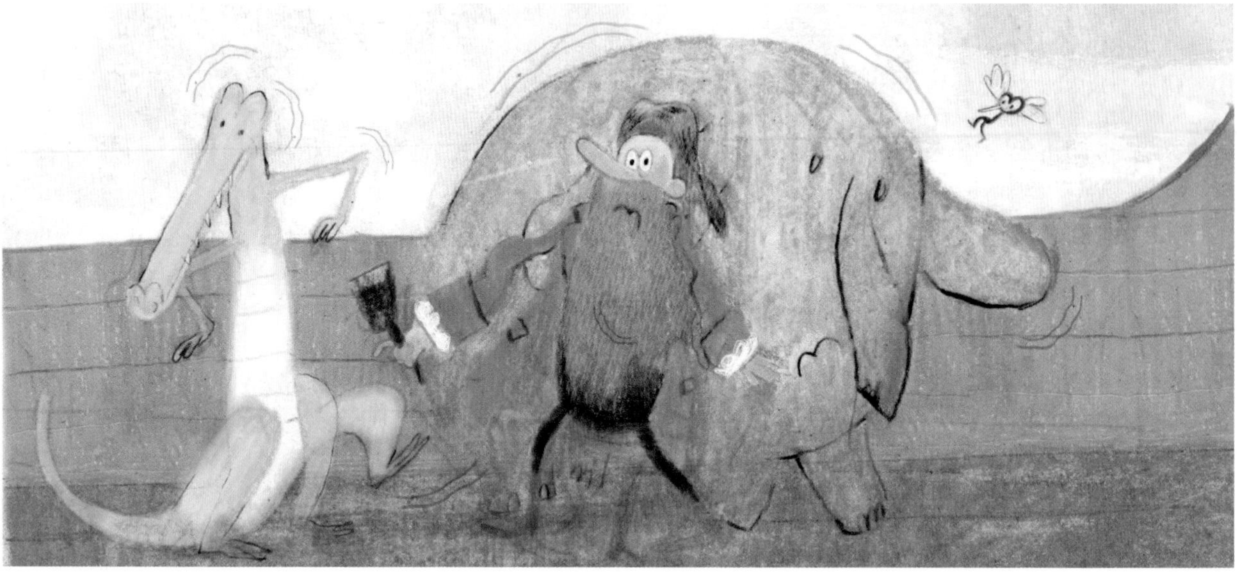

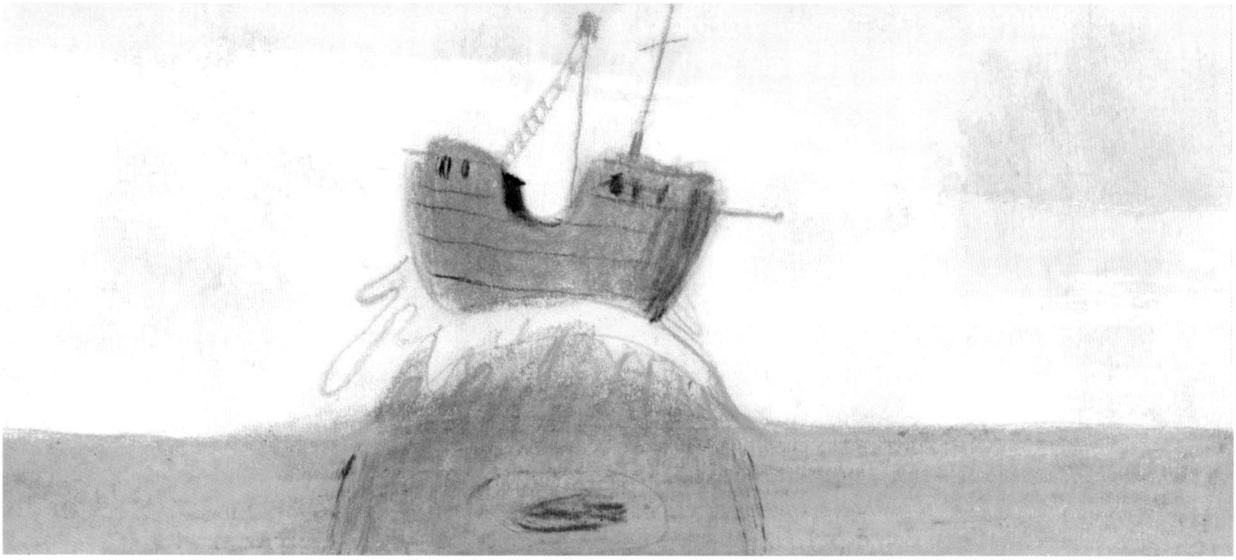

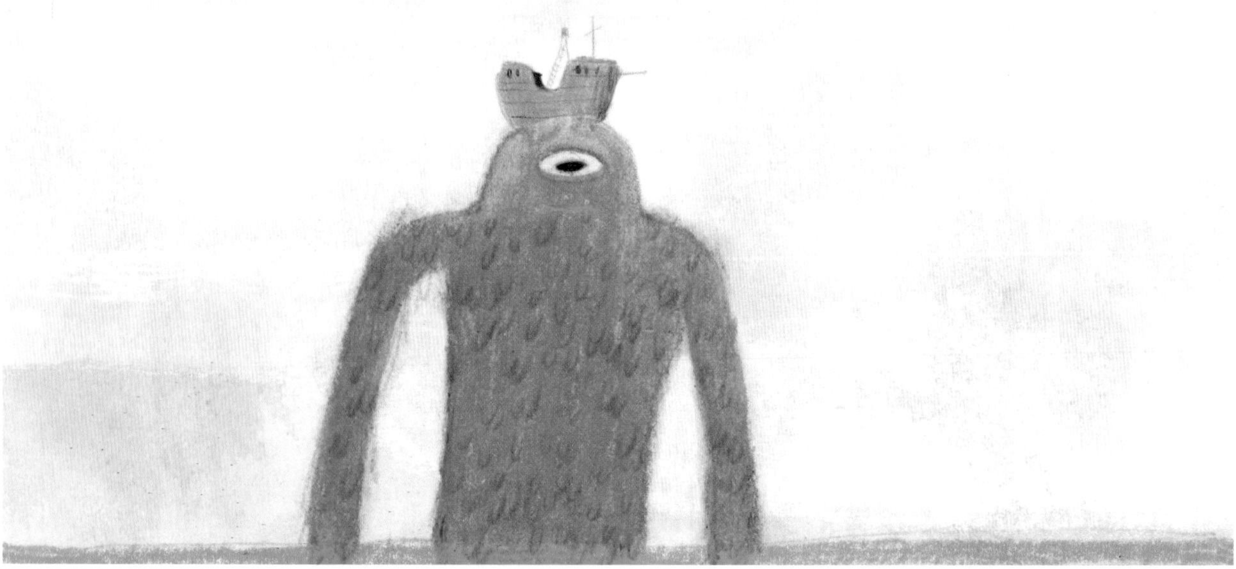

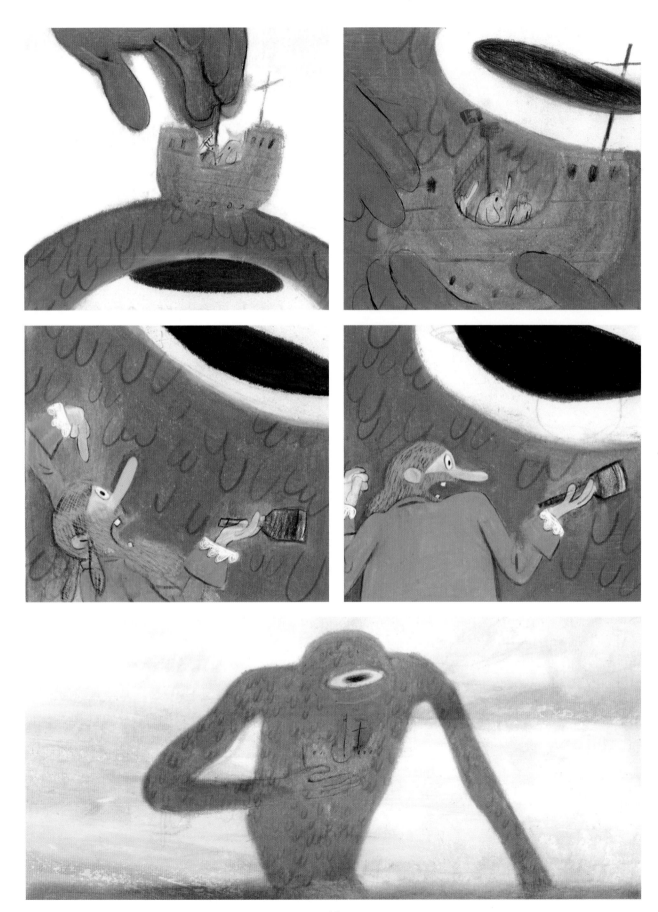

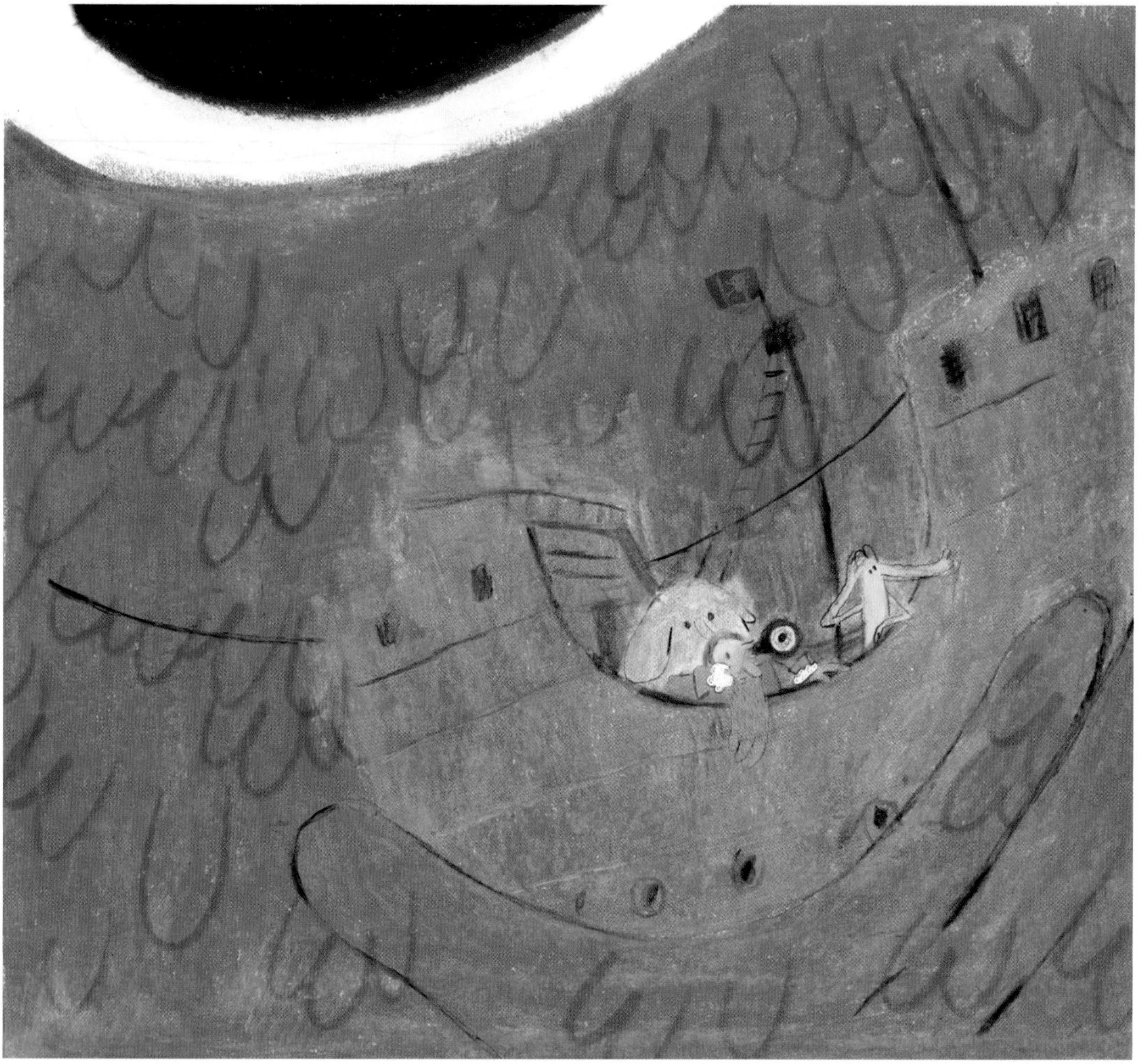

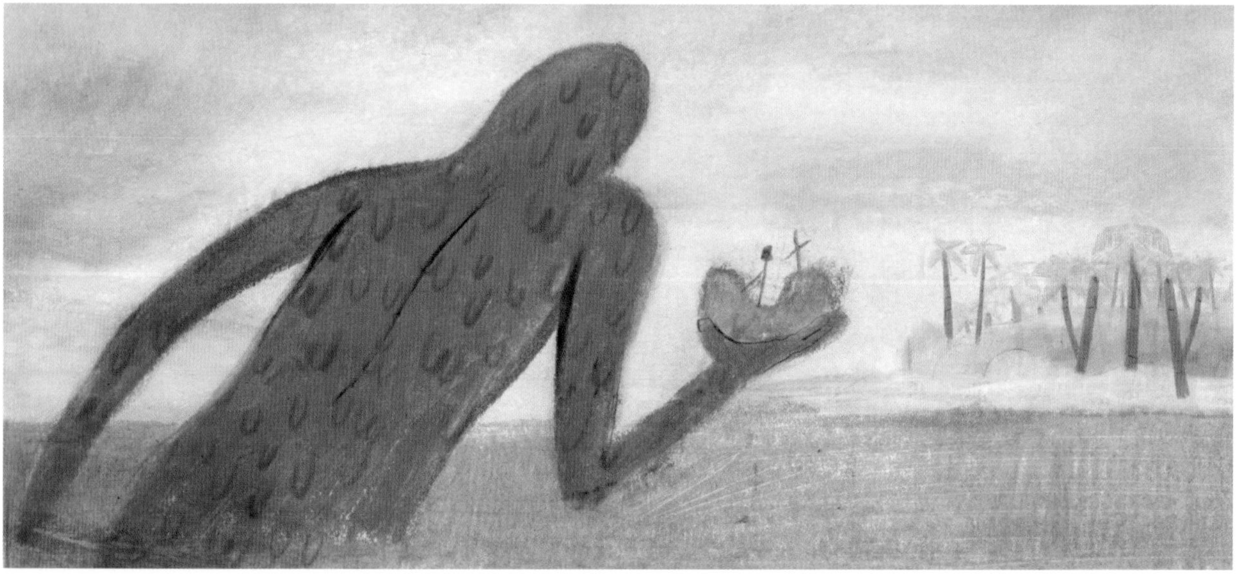

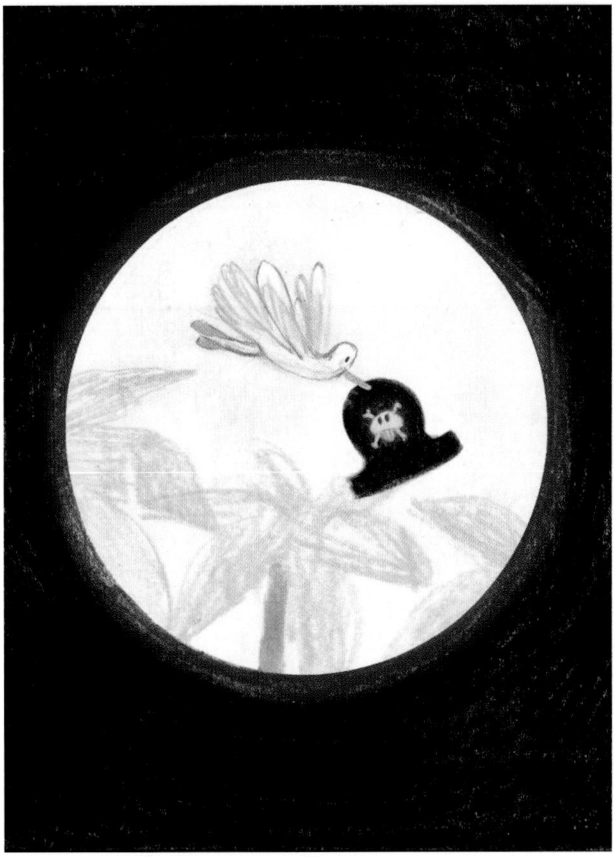
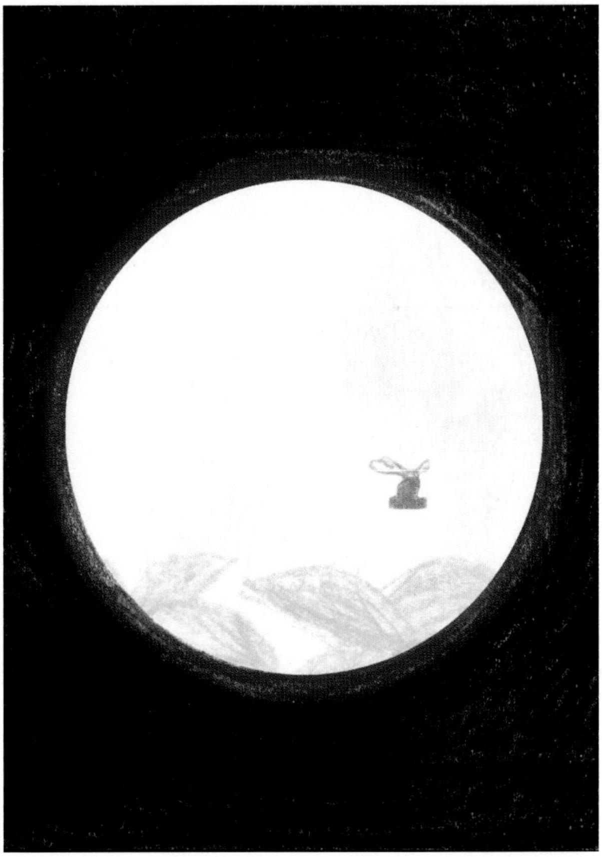
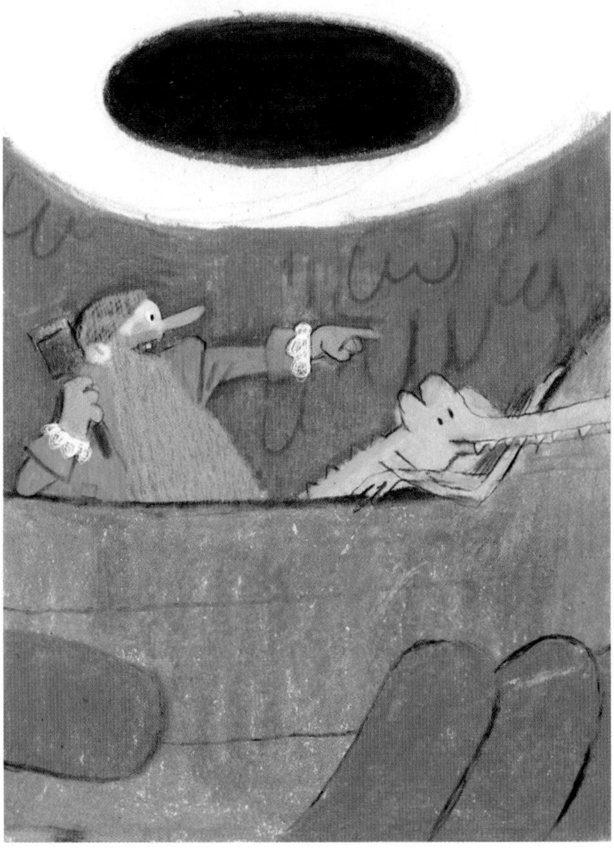
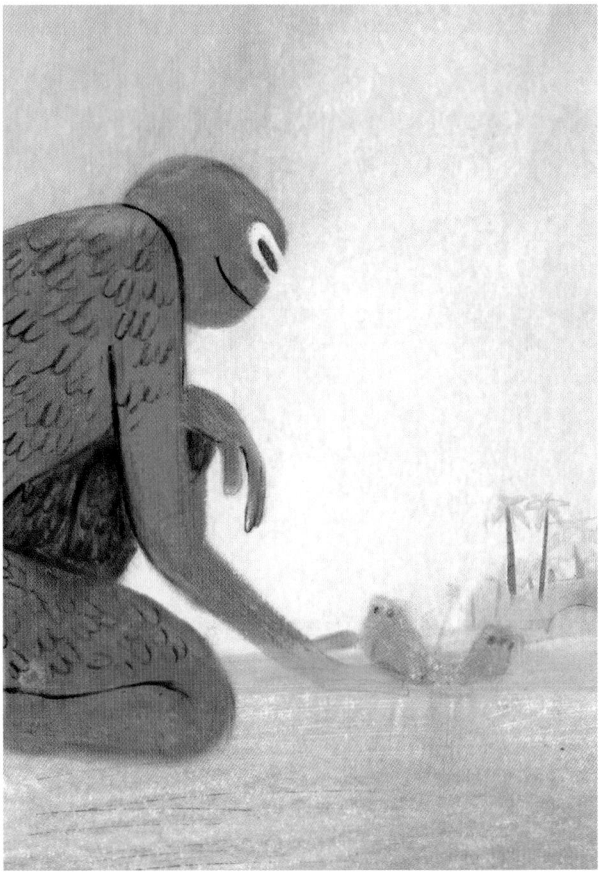

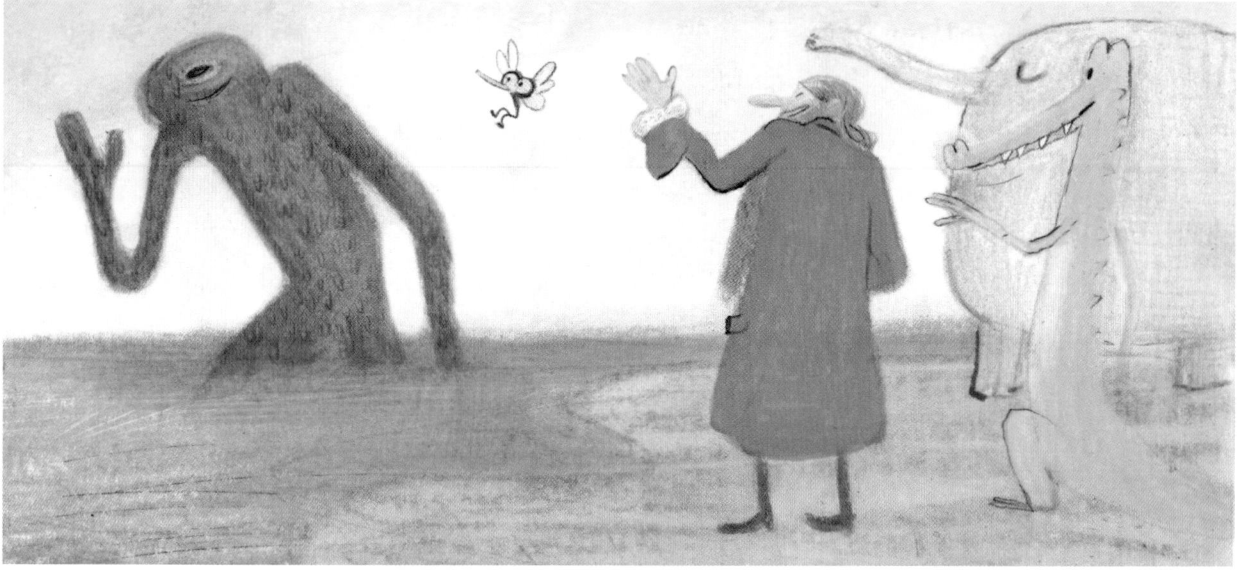

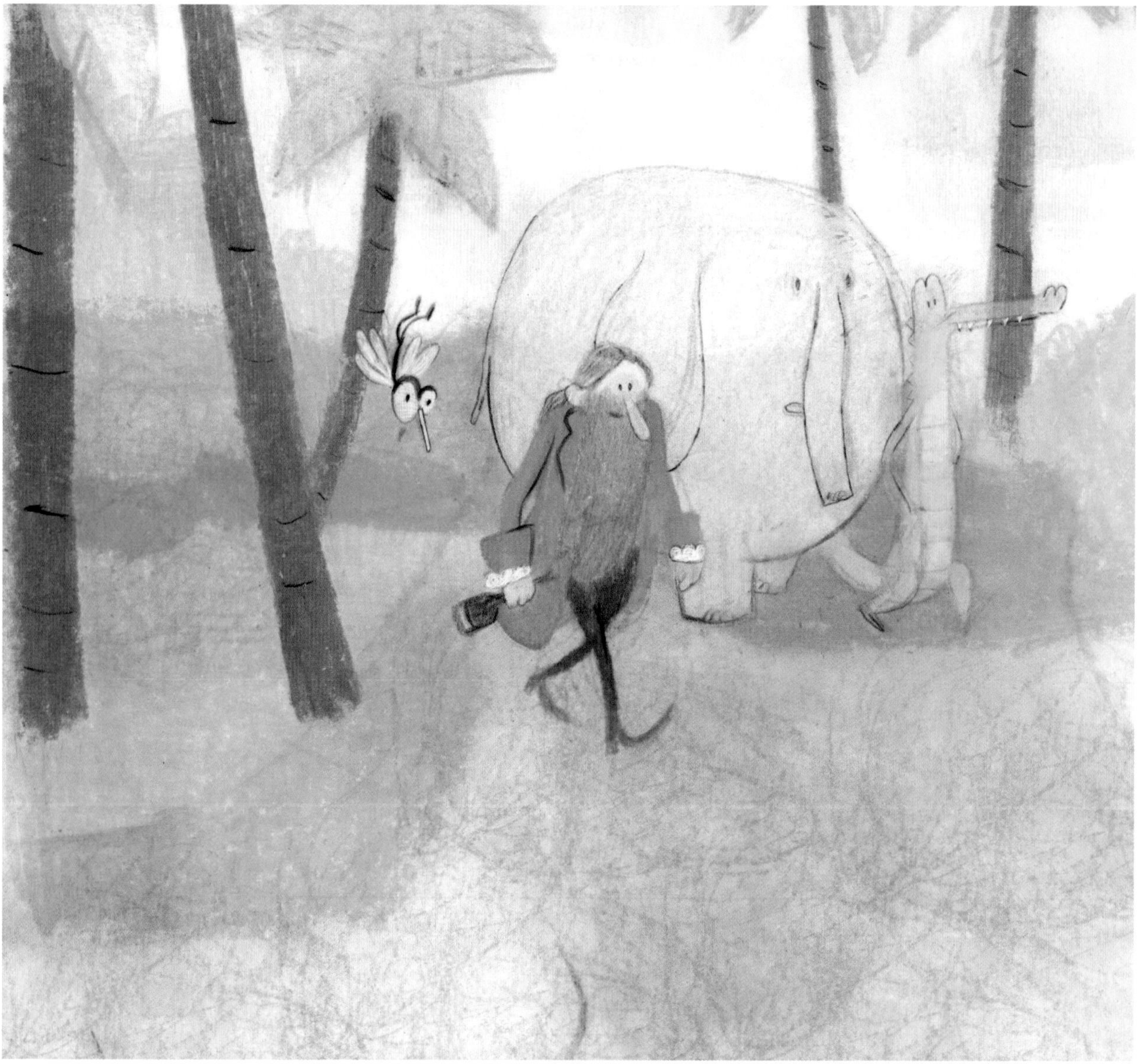

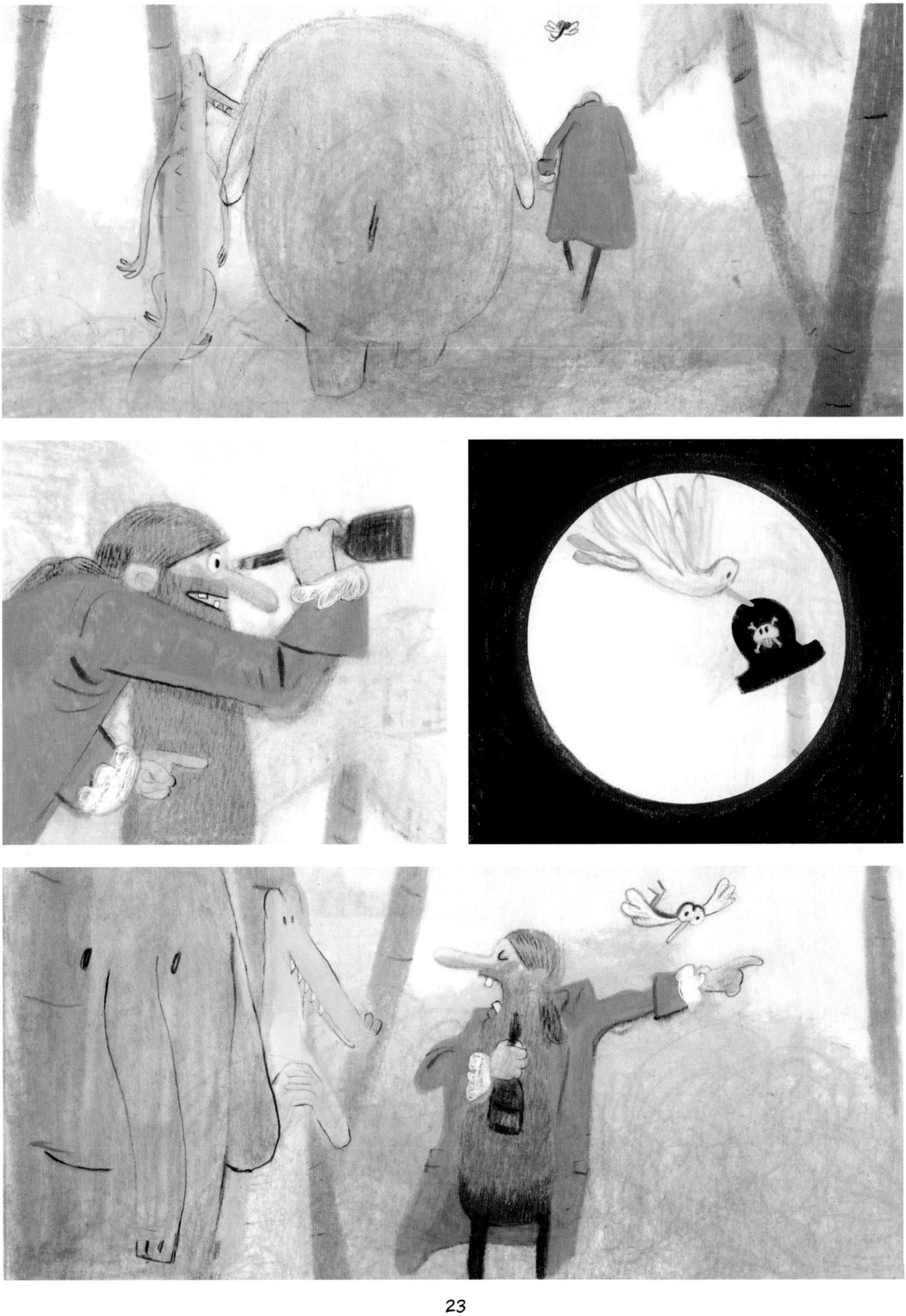

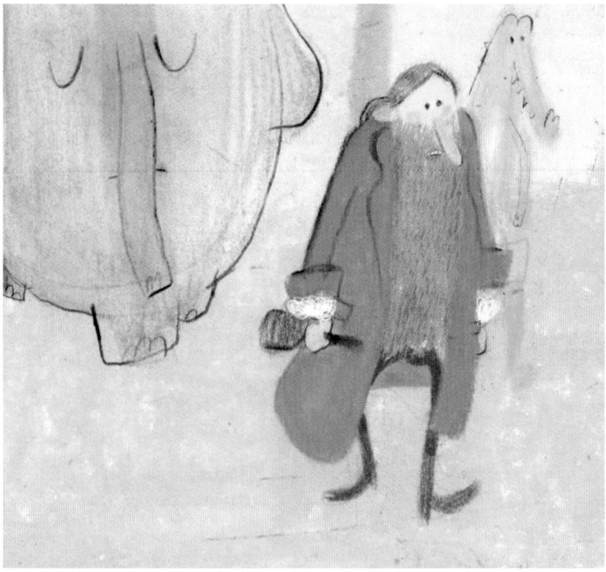

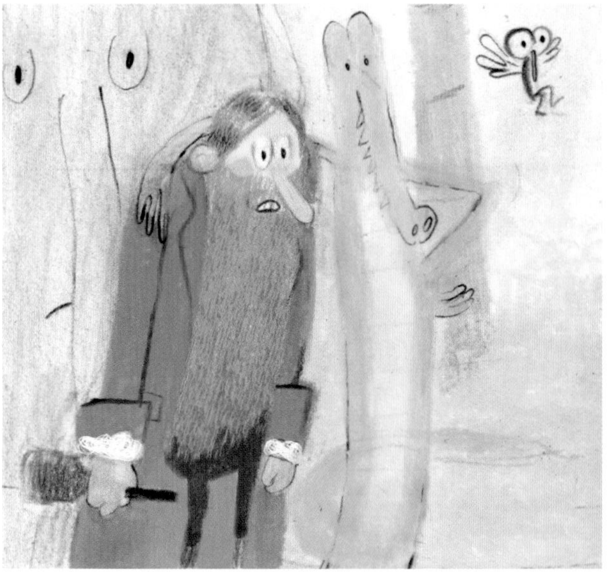

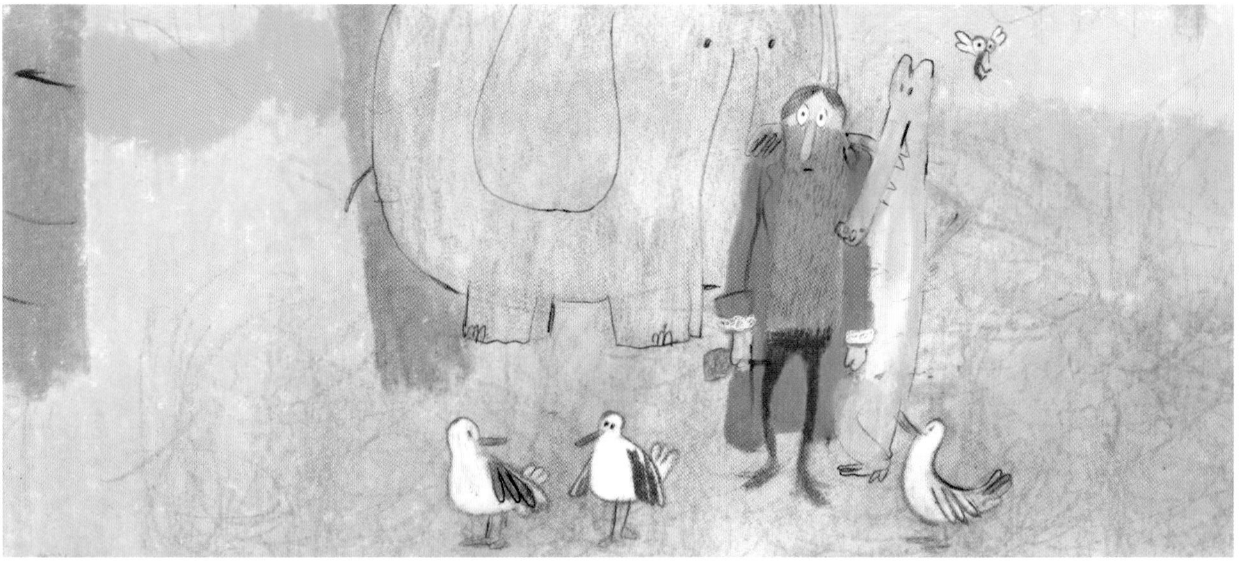

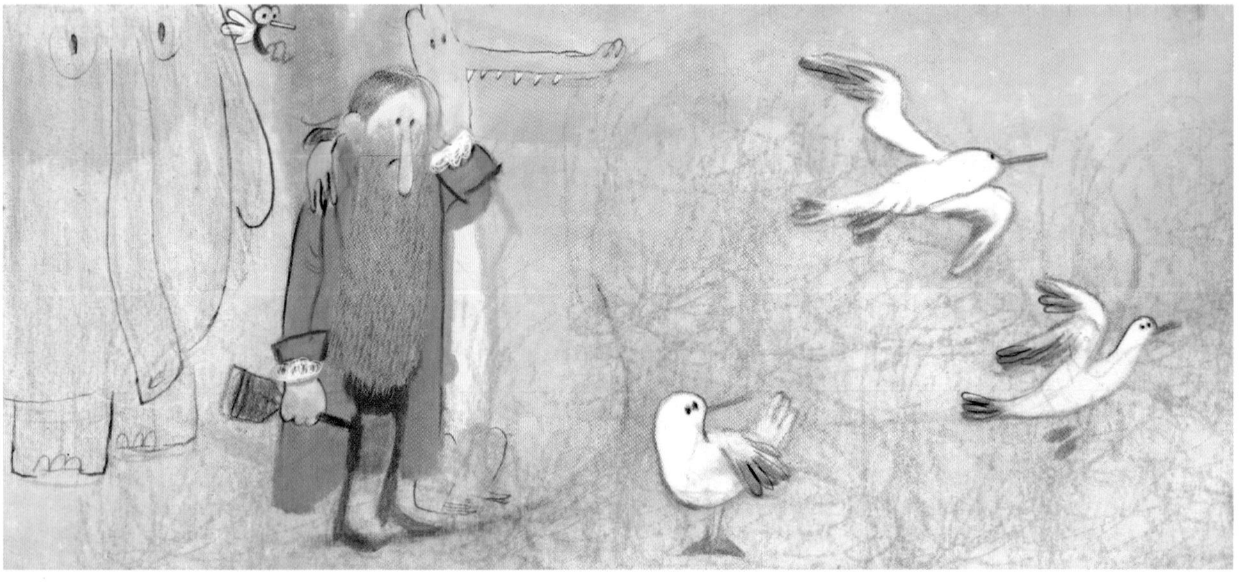

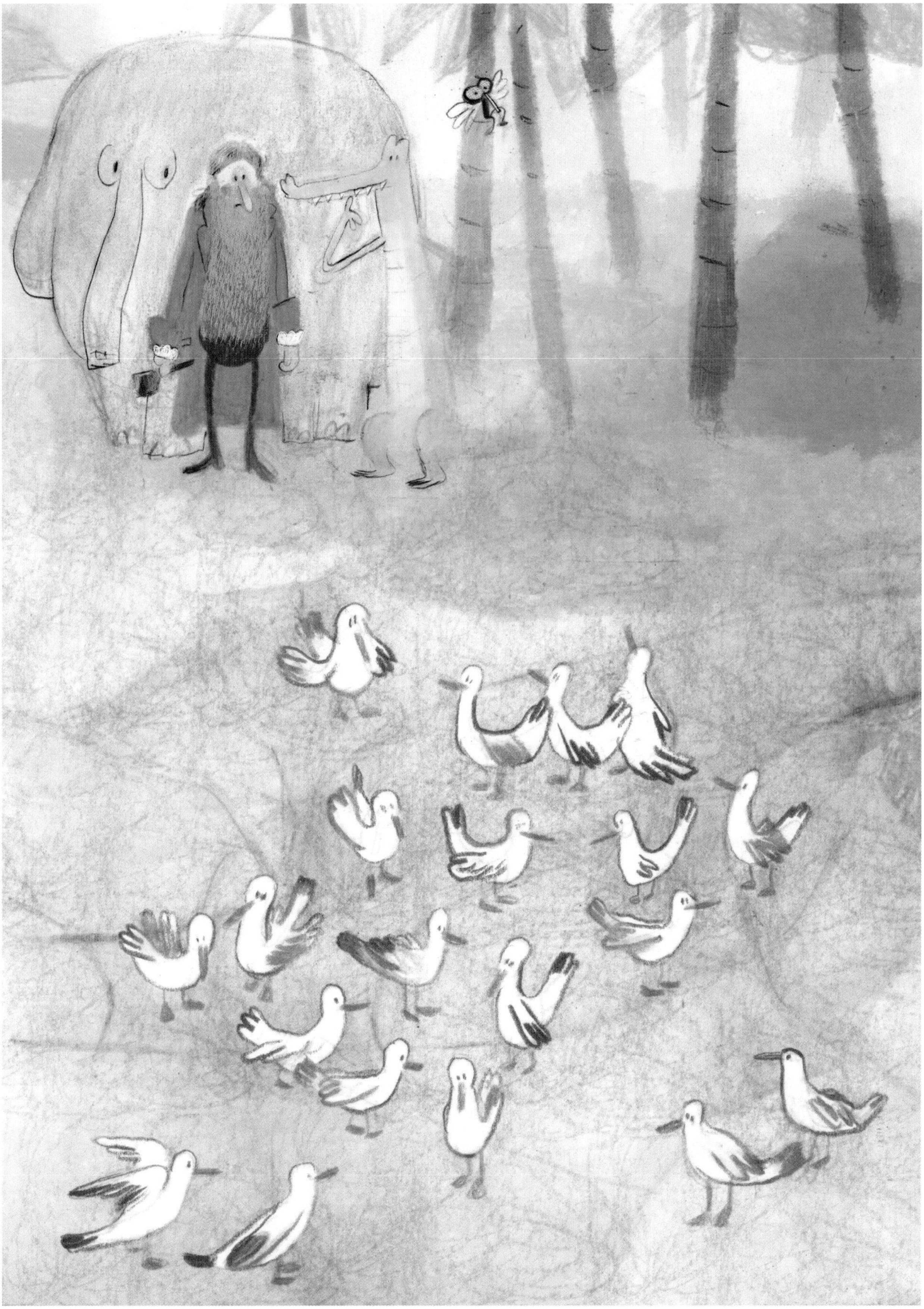

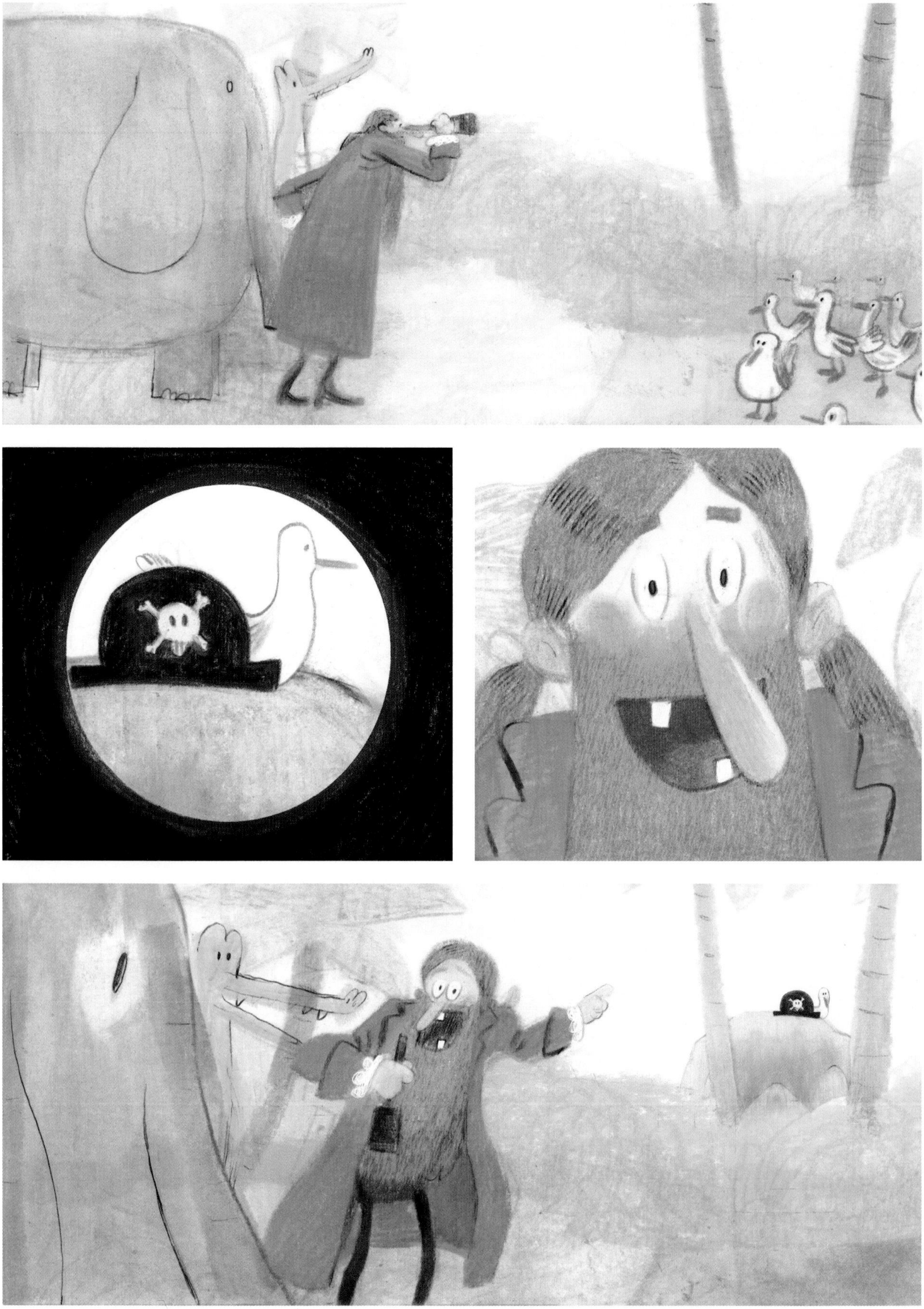

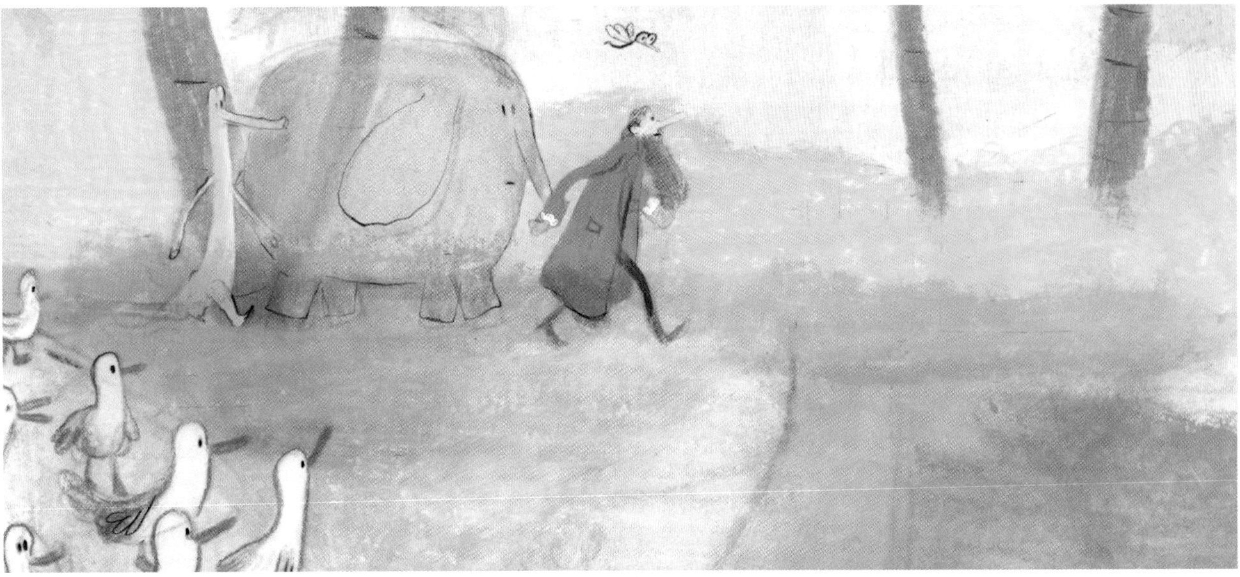

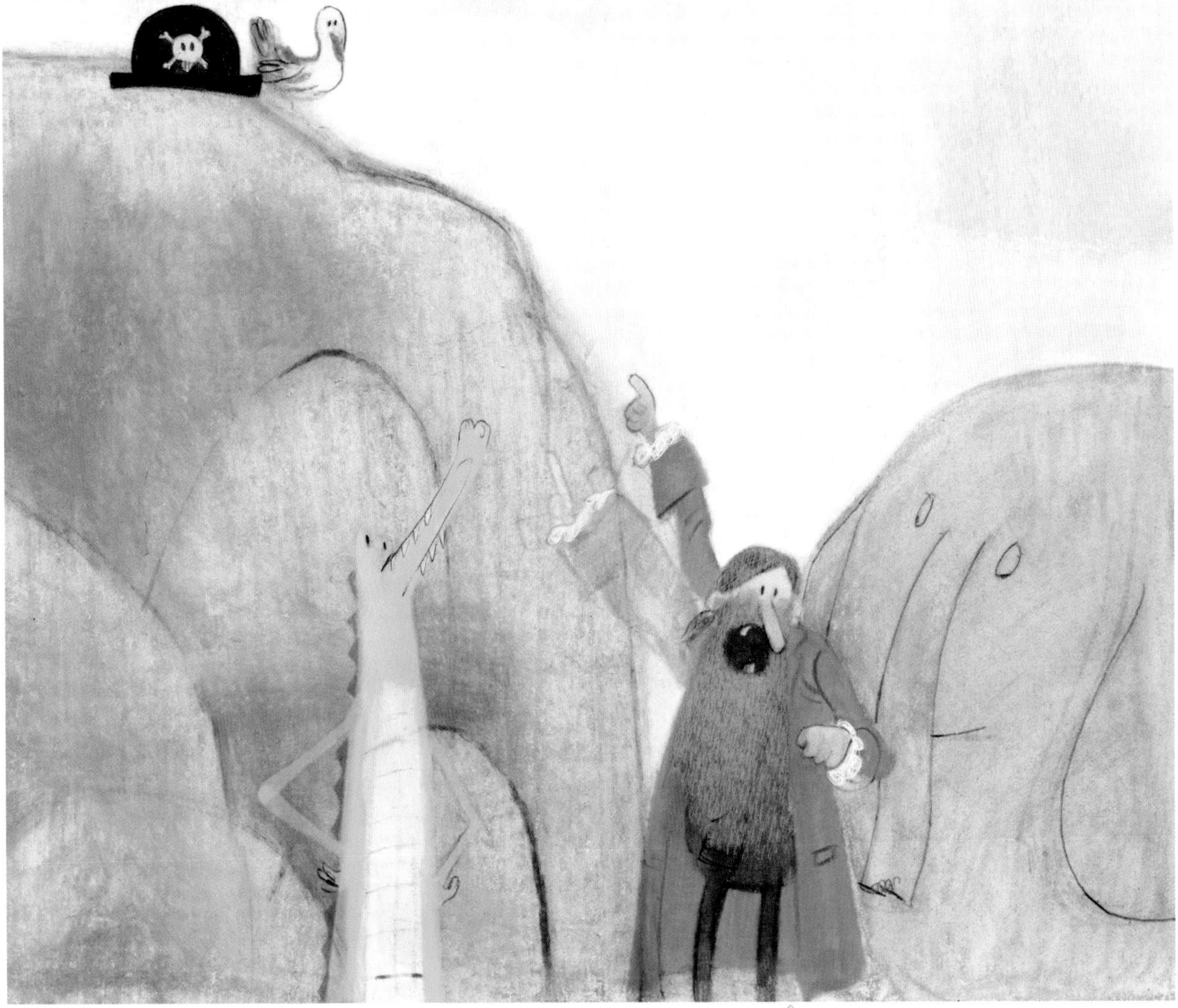

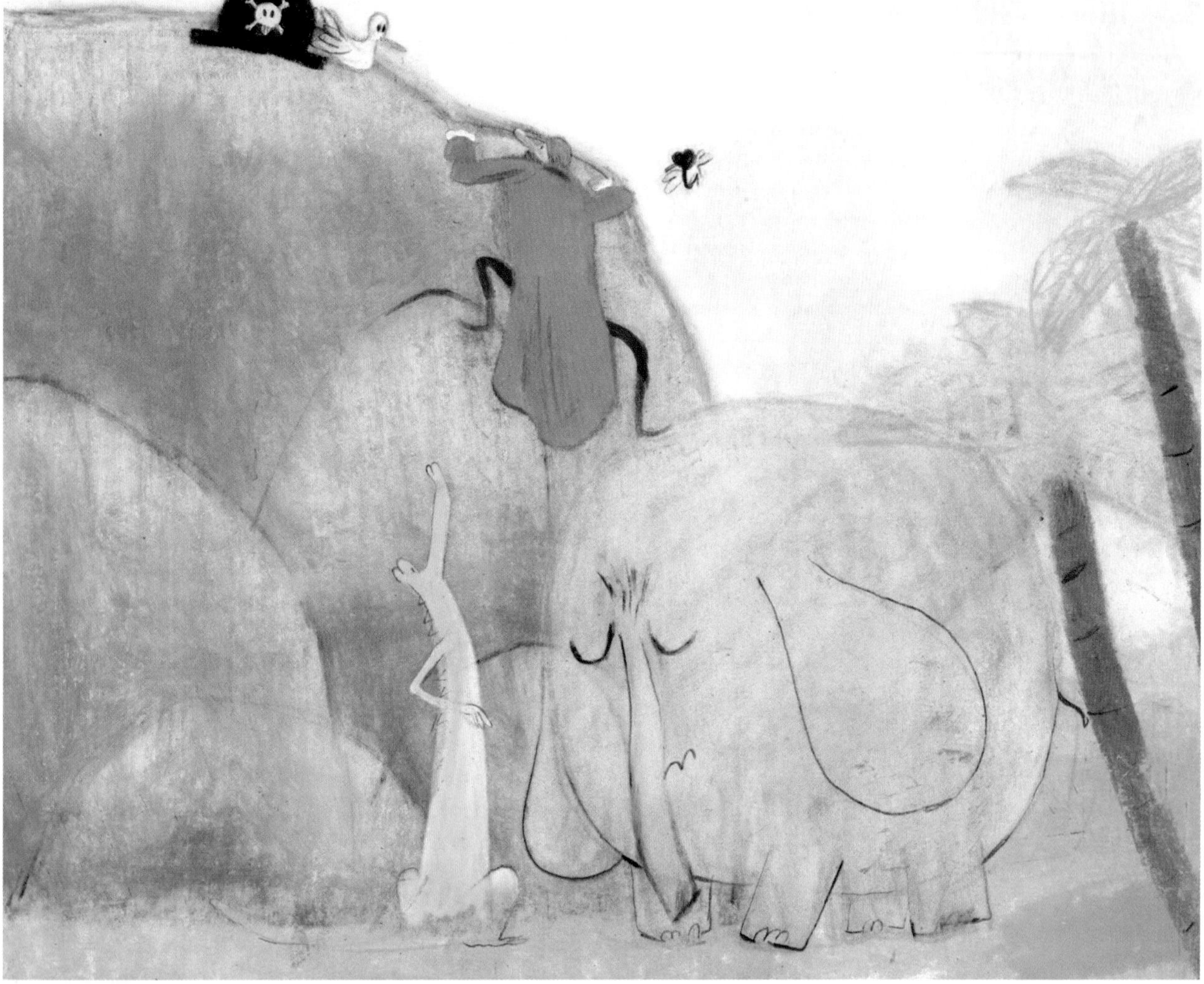

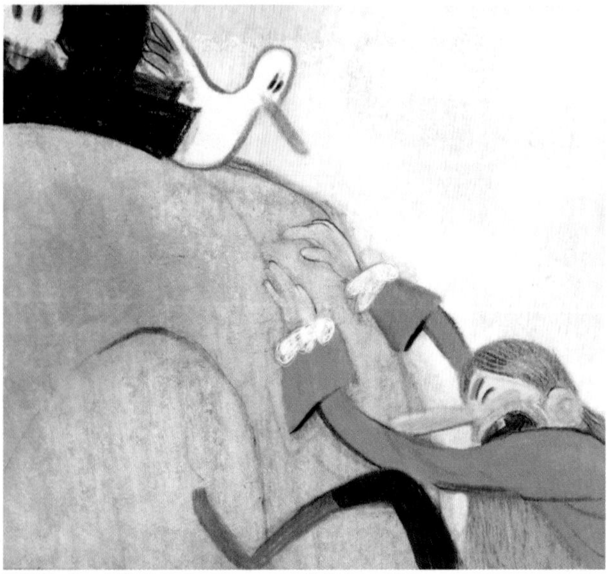

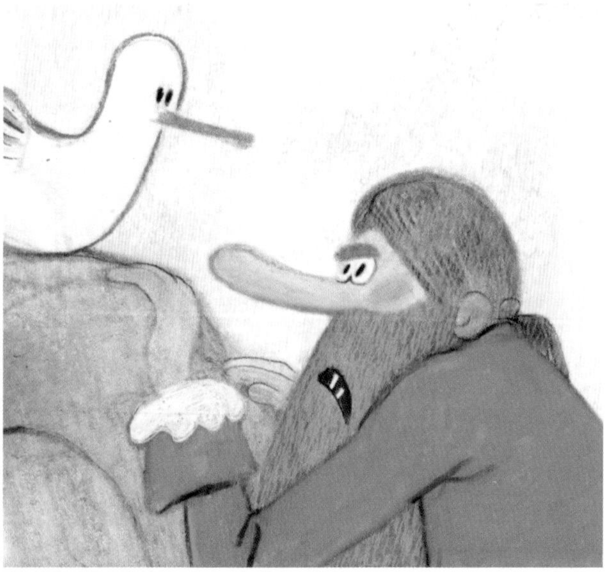

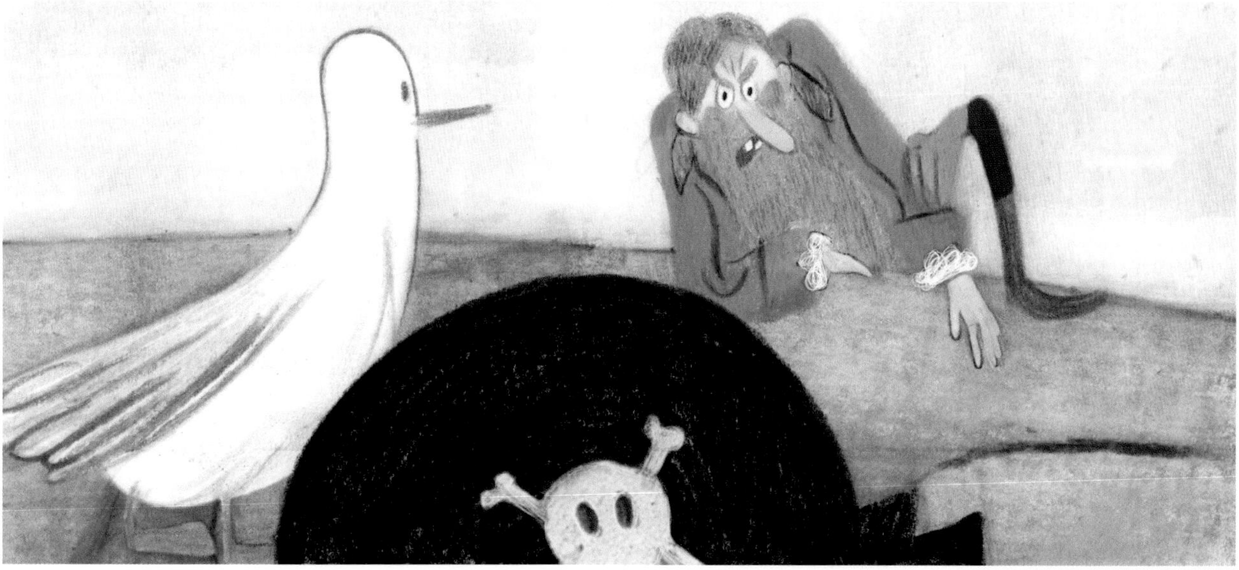

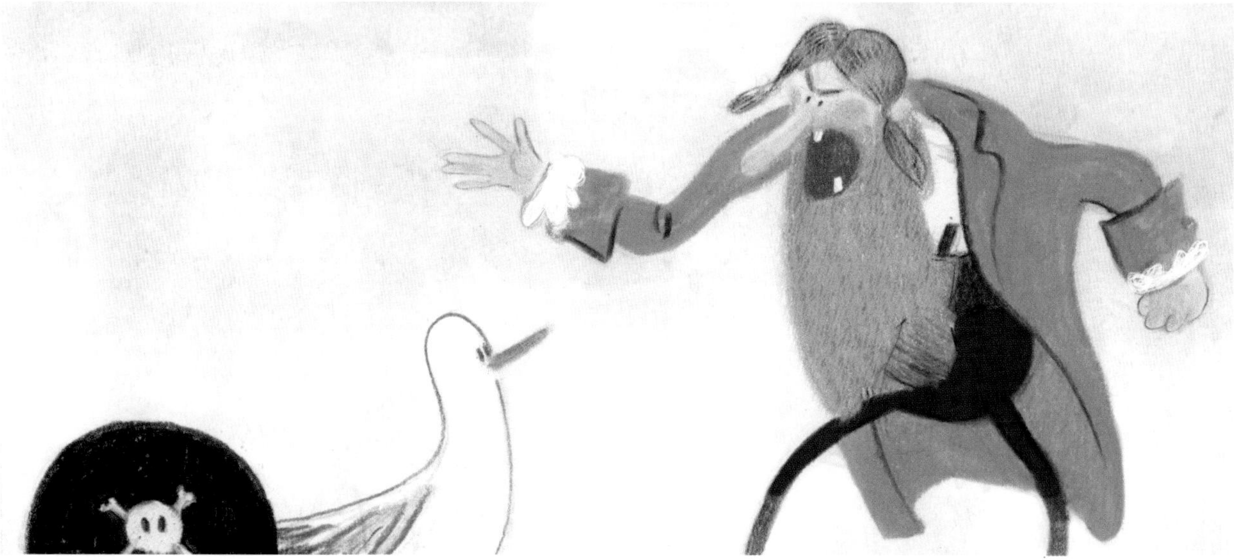

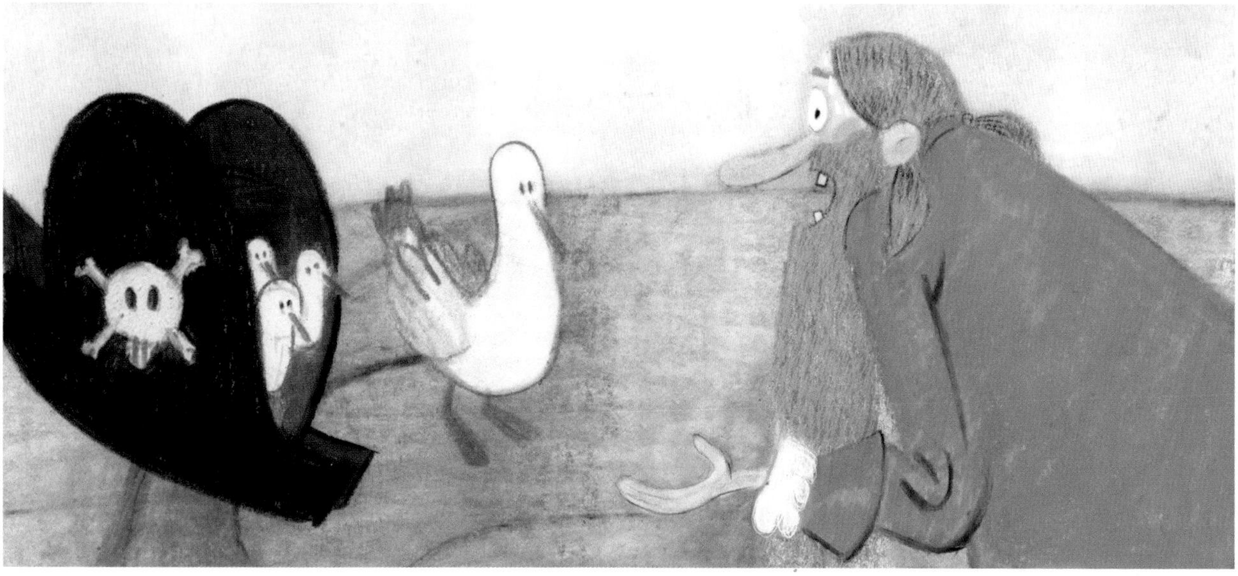

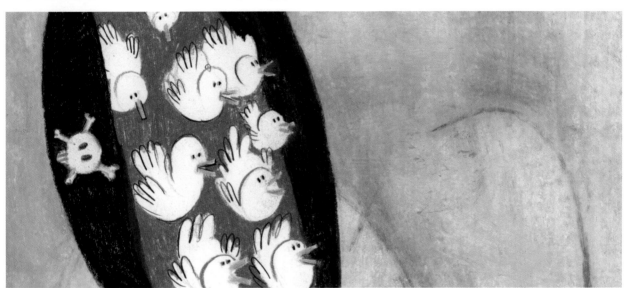

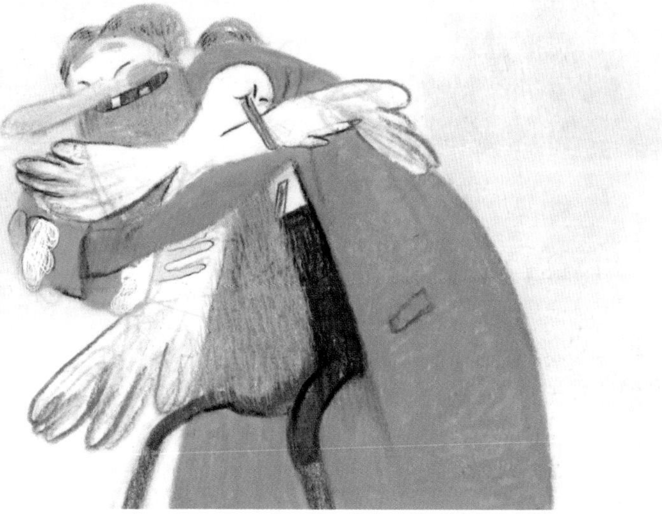

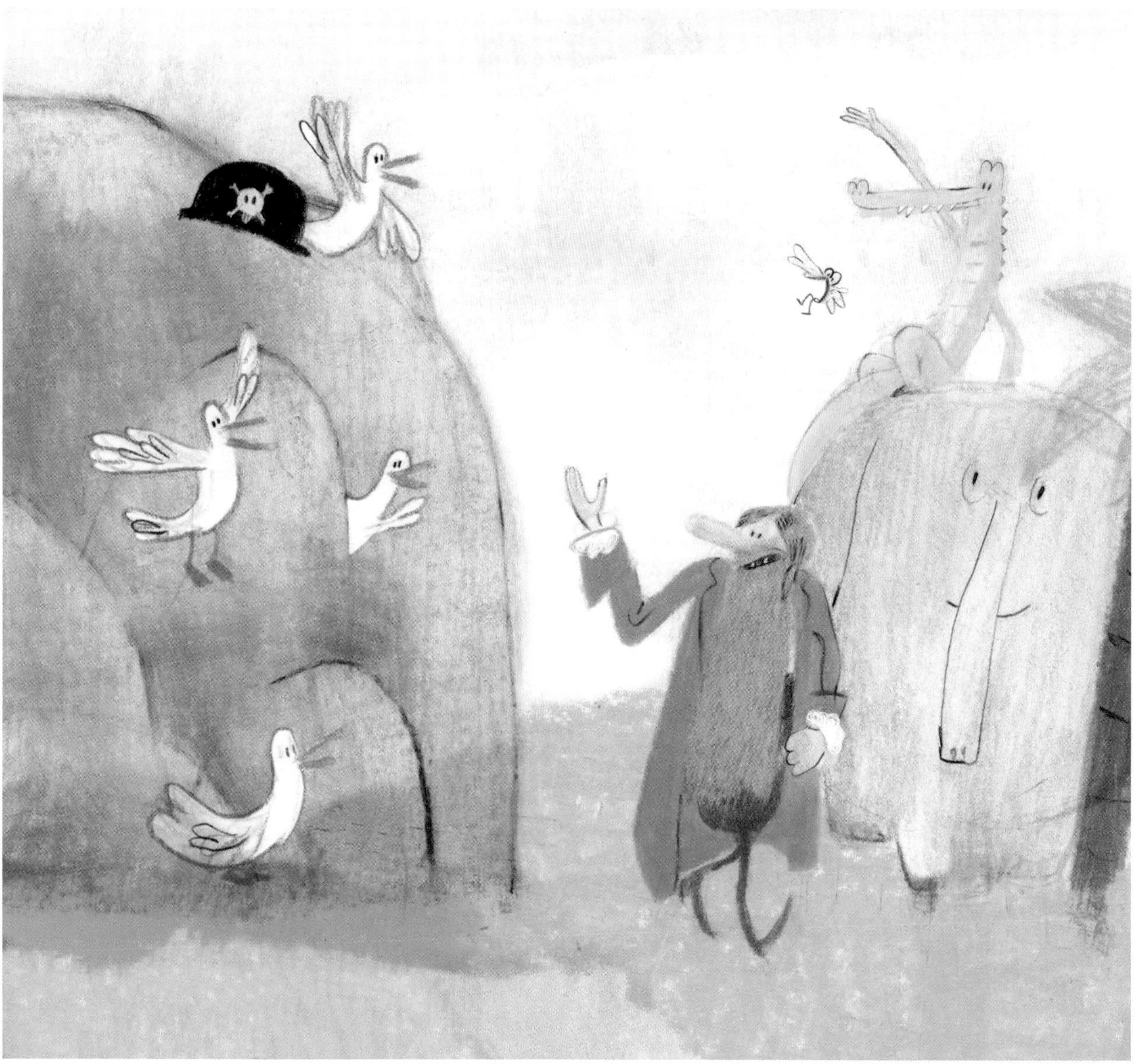

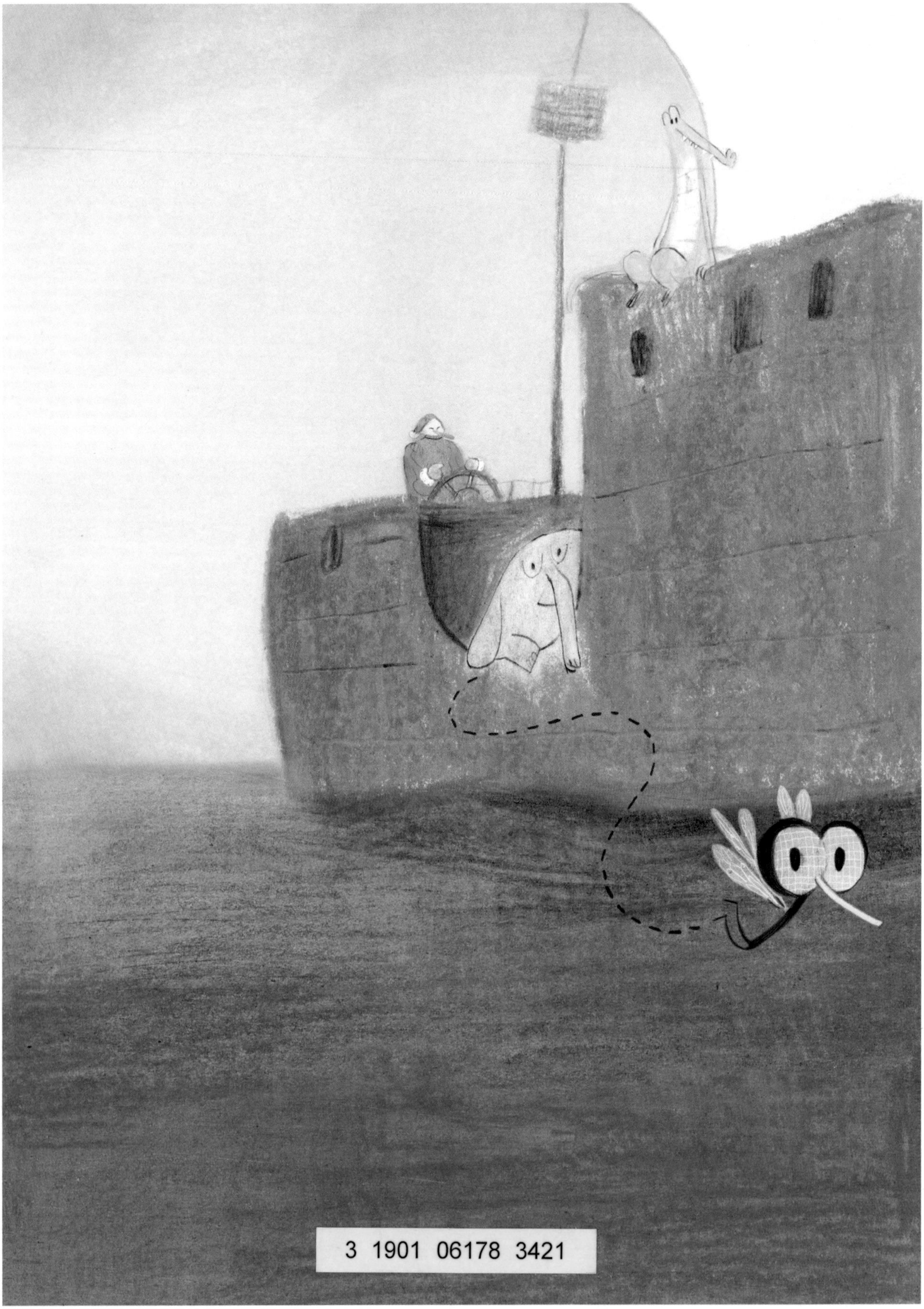